THE WITCHES OF AUBURN
A NOVELLA

HAZEL BLACK

Also by Hazel Black

THE WITCHES OF AUBURN SERIES

The Gifts of Our Mothers (Witches of Auburn, Book 1)
The Sins of Our Fathers (Witches of Auburn, Book 2)

THE WITCHES
OF AUBURN
A NOVELLA

Gisel

Brunswick House
New York

Brunswick House Publishing
244 Madison Avenue
New York, NY 10016
First Brunswick House ebook and print on demand edition: October 2017
The Brunswick House name and logo are trademarks of Brunswick House Publishing, LLC.
The publisher is not responsible for websites (or their content) that are not owned by the publisher.
Manufactured in the United States of America
ISBN 978–1-943622–13–9 (ebook edition)

ISBN 978–1-943622–11–5 (print on demand edition)

A coven in The Witches of Auburn *is born the same year through a bloodline destined to carry on the powers of the world. In real life, a coven is formed less theatrically, but no less magically, through time and space, profound luck, and shared experiences.*

This books is dedicated to Jill Kugler and Kate Waters with

honor
and love

and a fierce protection of the friendship we share.

This would be my only mistake.

Twenty years ago . . .

ISAIAH'S BODY TOOK UP MOST of the doorway. He leaned against the dingy white molding and rested his head on it. Without the doorjamb as a gauge, I'd never have believed he was the same height he'd been a few weeks ago. He certainly hadn't shrunk, but he still seemed smaller. His loss of stature wasn't physical, though. The emotional blow he took when Helene left seemed to cut him off at the knees.

He'd been here every day since that day, but I didn't know why. Maybe it was because he needed to talk to someone about her or maybe he just drifted back to the last place he'd seen her. From my house you could see up to her bedroom window and into her kitchen. Perhaps, Isaiah was as attracted to the memory of her as he'd been to Helene.

"Did you find her?" I asked, but I didn't really need to. If he'd been able to fix things by following Helene to Vermont, he wouldn't be standing in my kitchen in New Jersey right now. Based on the tortured look on his face, none of his possible answers would bring either of us any peace.

He nodded with his sight fixed on my mother's sun hat and gardening gloves, which rested in the center of the kitchen table. They were covered in soil and were out of place on the table. On a different day, she never would have left them there.

I filled two glasses with ice and poured vodka halfway up into both. The only juice in my refrigerator was orange, and I used it to top off the toxic concoctions. The glasses were freebies from McDonalds, and the colors had faded into an almost gray picture. I stirred the drinks and handed Isaiah the glass with the Hamburglar on it. He was the criminal in my head.

"Where's your mom?" Isaiah asked and took a big gulp from his glass. She was obviously gone. We wouldn't be standing around drinking in front of her. She would end our eighteen-year-long lives with a stare.

"My dad's in the hospital again. She's with him."

Isaiah didn't say, "I'm sorry." Those words we'd never say to each other again. Not for anything.

I focused on my mother's gloves and tried to move them with my mind. I bit my bottom lip as I willed the glove to fly across the room, but it stayed perfectly still and out of place.

"Helene was talking to some people . . . other students, I think." His gaze fixed on the contents of his glass. "She was standing in the hallway outside a lecture hall." He took another long sip.

I abandoned my efforts to move the gloves and sighed. He was going to hurt me. Whenever he mentioned her, he inflicted pain. I let him keep coming back and doing it over and over again because it hurt less than being alone. The inside of my head was more terrifying than my reality these days.

"Some guy was talking to her, and Helene was laughing as if he was hilarious." Isaiah stared back at me, waiting for me to say something that would repair this, but I'd accepted weeks ago that this was our new reality. "Like she could be happy. Like she *was* happy." He wasn't angry or yelling. The two of us were too pathetic for that type of display.

"Did you talk to her? What did she say?" Why couldn't she just talk to him?

"She stared right at me and stopped laughing. Like a fireball had flown across her face. She didn't just stop smiling. She died in front of me. Every sign of life drained from her expression."

I'd told him to stop holding out hope a million times since Helene had moved to Vermont early for college just to avoid us. "Then what happened?"

"I thought she was going to talk to me, even if just to yell at me, but she excused herself and walked out." Isaiah's shoulders slumped farther. His head fell back as his empty stare connected with the ceiling. He might stand in my kitchen like this forever because he had no idea how to move forward without her.

"And?" I couldn't take it anymore. The silence screamed at me from everywhere, but mostly in my head where the voices of my sisters no longer spoke to me. It didn't matter how often I called out to each of them every day or begged them to answer me—there was nothing.

"She disappeared. I sat outside her dorm like a criminal for three hours, but she never came back. No one would talk to me about her." He stood straight. "She must have already warned them that if I ever came by they weren't supposed to tell me a thing about her."

"Of course, that's the only explanation for a girl not telling you exactly what you want."

Isaiah downed his drink. I followed his lead. We'd drink ourselves through our first semester at college and forget about the loves we'd lost. I refilled our glasses, but there wasn't enough vodka in the world to make me forget Helene and Lovie and Sloane.

We escaped the kitchen—the scene of my second crime against my coven—and sat on the plastic chairs perched in my backyard, which was where we drank three more screwdrivers. I made all the drinks, but I couldn't tell you how we finished the bottle. It'd seemed like only an hour ago I'd cracked the seal on the bottle, and now I handed it to Isaiah to hide behind the seat in his pickup. Mama hated alcohol, especially when Daddy drank it.

"Let's go for a ride, and we'll throw it out at Wawa." There was nothing better to do. The isolation was drilling a hole in my soul.

Isaiah barely stayed on his side of the road, but there were no other cars to demand his composure. We drove out past Upper Pittsgrove and swung back around through Woodstown. When the darkness finally replaced every glimmer of hope in the sky, he pulled behind hay bales, which were stacked two stories high on the edge of a field. They formed a wall between Isaiah's truck and the world outside that had rendered us angry and bitter.

"Did you bring me here thinking I'd have sex with you again?" I was practically slurring. I sat straight in his truck to mask the effects of the vodka.

"Are you kidding?" he asked. His expression held nothing but hate. I couldn't tell if it was directed at him or me. "I can barely stand the sight of you." He pursed his lips together.

The memory of his hands touching me, pulling me down against him while his lips pressed so hard on mine I thought I'd bleed ran through my mind. It was followed by the familiar guilt scraping my insides in its wake.

"Let's climb the wall," he said and got out of the truck.

I stayed still in my seat. The hay was stacked straight up with an uneven amount on each row, creating a staircase on one side. No one should climb it. I could have flown. I swallowed down the longing for the gifts of my old life.

Isaiah opened my door, leaned against it, and stared at me until I rolled my eyes and followed him to the hay. By the third row, the bales beneath us were unsteady. Each row was designed to support the one above it. Not me and my best friend's enormous ex-boyfriend.

Isaiah held each bale above me as I climbed before him. He was a gentleman and kind and had no business being anywhere near me. He'd ruined my life. I'd ruined his. The liquor clouded my judgment. Again.

The breeze picked up on the top row. I stayed in the middle of the stack and let my hair blow across my face. It was as close to flying as I'd come in months. The farthest I'd been off the ground. My intoxication morphed into adoration for the sky and the air and the night. It was my home. I'd owned it with my coven, but it was lost to me.

"Gisel . . . what are you doing?"

I could barely hear him; I was fixated on the night around me. "Maybe they'd come back if it was a life-or-death situation." *Once a witch, always a witch.*

"The girls? Are you talking about Helene and Lovie and Sloane?"

I'd given up on them. There was nothing left to say. Not a word they'd hear. They may as well have been dead. I'd be better off if they were. "No. I'm talking about my powers." I leaned farther into the breeze and stepped to the end of the bale. The straw gave way at the edges and released from the tightly knotted rectangle. I played with the frayed straw with the toe of my shoe. "I've never been without them."

"Or the girls."

"It's so sad." I didn't feel like crying, though. My anger kept me alive. It would make me fly again. "All of it. Incredibly tragic. My entire life gone in one day."

Isaiah stared at me as I spoke. The moonlight barely lit his face enough to see the pity. I was pathetic. I turned away from him and my old life, bent my knees, and swung my hands into the air. I—

Isaiah tackled me onto the hay beneath us. He landed on top of me and held me there. The weight of him, the length of his body, and the memories of the last time he was there, forced a tear to break through my frozen interior.

"You still have power, Gisel," he whispered in my ear. "You weren't just a witch, and you're not just a girl now."

"You're only being nice."

"I'm being your friend."

He rolled to my side, and I sat up facing him. "You should have been my friend that night."

"I know."

"I absolutely *hate* you. The only person I deplore more than myself is you, Isaiah Kennedy. You're the worst human being to ever walk the face of this earth."

"You repulse me, too." He lay back and stared and the night sky.

"I mean . . ." My head shook. Something in my core was breaking free. It was either because of the vodka or his touch. "What were we thinking? How could we?"

"I can't talk about it or I'll jump myself."

The thought of him erased from the situation pleased me. "I should push you. Helene will forgive me if I kill you."

"No, she won't."

"We should give it a try."

The solution doesn't exist in hatred.

Four years later . . .

"WHAT DO YOU THINK OF her?" I asked Ike, who was secure on Isaiah's lap at the edge of my hospital bed.

Ike leaned over until his little nose almost touched his new sister's. He was solid. Even as a one-year-old, Ike rarely showed big emotions either way. Yet, this little baby his father and I had been talking about for months intrigued him.

"En?"

"Yes. She's Gwen." He was working on the first sounds of lots of words. "Isn't she lovely?" The powerful energy filled me. More air entered my lungs. I inhaled the aroma of bread pudding and could tell by the squeak in the wheel that the dinner cart was a few doors down. I tilted my chin up and let my head fall back to take in the activity around me. I was a witch again, and I knew it was because this little girl in my arms was one, too. My powers had been reborn with my daughter on November eighth.

Isaiah pulled Ike against his chest. He wrapped his arms tight around his son as if he could sense the world falling around us and stirring the dormant powers inside me. I wanted to dress her in black lace to take her home and adorn the car with feathers. I could fly with her and speak to her inside her head. Every cemented doubt that came with the birth of Ike—a boy who'd never be a witch—was erased with the addition of Gwen to our family.

I didn't know it in my hospital bed, but that sense of possibility was fleeting. In the weeks after we brought Gwen home, I wasn't sure if the feeling had been imagined at her birth or erased the second we'd entered our house as parents of two children. I spent my days with Ike and Gwen, caring for both of them like any *normal* mother, but at the same time attempting to move things with my mind, calling out to my lost coven in my head, and trying to capture the fleeting energy that rested beneath my skin and focused under the pads of my fingers the day Gwen had been born.

The hint of power faded. I knew what was left was the memory of it and not an actual ability. Gwen developed like the girls in her infant swim class at the YMCA. They all looked divinely adorable and frustratingly similar. My daughter was not just a girl. She was a *witch*. It was her birthright, and I wouldn't let it be stolen from her the way it'd been taken from me.

February twenty-third was the next day I had hope. Gwen was strapped into her bouncy chair while she watched puppets singing on the television. She kicked her legs and shook her hands along to the music. I should have signed her up for a baby music class, but the thought of the other mothers kept me from registering. They were all so impressed with their babies. So complacent. Their company made me feel like a bad mother, or maybe it highlighted the evidence that I was. Either way, I chose to just sing to her as much as possible because I couldn't be around the other mothers.

Ike loved cartoons, too. Especially the television show where the dinosaur pranced around the playground singing about sharing. On that day, Ike was standing next to Gwen's seat and shaking his little tushy in her face, taunting Gwen like a big brother.

He reached down and swiped the stuffed lamb from her bouncy seat. Gwen froze. She glared at Ike, who tucked the lamb under his armpit and made some grunting sound. Ike stuck his tongue out at her before turning back to the television and dancing again.

I waited for him to regret the transgression or for Gwen to wail, but instead, a book flew from the shelf, soared across the room, and hit Ike right between the eyes. It fell to the ground with a thud that made it impossible to assign an explanation to its flight. Ike's hands covered his head, and Gwen's lamb flew right into her lap. She held it to her face and pulled it close to her body before returning to her dance.

Ike didn't cry. He was a tough kid. He turned away from the show and his sister. I brushed his hair off his forehead and looked him in each eye, searching for any sign of distress or pain. He smiled in his sweet little way before he found his toy cars in the corner of the room and played alone the rest of the morning.

I took an index card from the desk and wrote February twenty-third on it before taping it to the inside of the cabinet door that held all of my cookbooks. No one ever looked in there, not even me. That night, I bundled into my parka and stood at the lake's edge. Isaiah had wanted to buy our house. He loved to be near the water. I'd wanted to stay in Auburn. I felt safe there. If my powers were going to return, they'd find me on the banks of the crick in Auburn, New Jersey, not on the lake in Alloway.

He'd won. Sometimes, I felt like he always won. Isaiah had convinced me to marry him and move and have his babies. I was certain of his will until he was asleep next to me in our bed. In the quiet darkness, I had to admit to myself that most of those things I'd done. Helene had left Isaiah as weak as she'd rendered me. He was lost without her and somewhat malleable. I could barely see three feet in front of me and had clung to Isaiah because he was the only person left who truly knew me. Even the parts of me that shouldn't exist.

The wind whipped over the surface of the lake and across my face. I closed my eyes and took the abuse.

"Today could be every day," a husky feminine voice behind me said. The chill from the words straightened my spine and pressed my feet into the frozen ground. "Gisel, you could be whole again."

I swung around, but there wasn't anyone there. At least not that I could see. "Who are you? Where are you?"

The remnants of a slight chuckle reached my ears. "You know us. You've been waiting for us." *The Virago*. The witches who couldn't make it in a coven. The outcasts. A bunch of bitter women who toyed with innocent people's lives to stave off boredom.

"What do you want?"

"Only what's best for you. We can give you your power back."

"I don't know what you're talking about."

Her laugh echoed through the trees. "Oh, Gisel, I know you do."

Just for a moment, I wanted to talk about the chance of my powers returning. I longed to lay down and feel them invade me. "How can you return my powers?" I was ignoring my caution and letting go of every lecture my mother had ever given me about the Virago and their diseased existence.

"There are a few among us who have become a coven of one. They've successfully created new covens, and we could use an Earth witch."

"No thanks." I snapped back from my need and returned to my roots. I was not a witch who would ever consider the Virago my coven or even my friends. Those witches were crazy.

"You've been alone for years. It's time to be born again."

"I'd rather die."

"Then why haven't you killed yourself?" Her breath brushed against my earlobe. "I thought you were close on a few occasions, but you're still here. Hoping they'll come back?" I didn't know if she meant my powers or my coven, but either way, I'd go it alone before aligning with the Queen of Hate next to me. "They're gone forever." She's lucky I had no powers. I'd bash her head into the icy lake if it meant she would stop talking.

"Leave and don't bother returning," I said and climbed the hill to my house. I may not be a witch, but I was still not one of them. The air lightened with her departure.

My family still lingered around the kitchen table. Isaiah was coloring with Ike as Gwen sat in her car seat between their artwork. Isaiah would break from his drawing to rock her or touch her hand every few moments.

"Where were you?" he asked without looking up.

I took off my coat and hung it on the hook by the back door. "I went down by the lake."

"Gisel, please don't get your hopes up." This was the reason for the sudden father-of-the-year coloring routine. He was pulling them close to him to shield them from my obsession. My old hate of Isaiah came back, but I forced it down. I hid it under the knowledge that I deserved better than this relationship. I exhaled and shook my head before facing him.

"I know. I'm fine. *It's* fine. Really." He stared at me with eyes full of distrust. "Just a nice normal family. One boy. One . . ." I swallowed back hope. "Girl."

The week of March sixth was unseasonably warm, and the daffodils in the front beds bloomed early. I'd been prancing around in tank tops, shorts, and flip-flops for almost a week and loved it. The warm weather always made me feel young, and with the ways of my youth came the recollection of how fabulous I used to be. I commanded the sky and the water, the fire and the earth. I was the center of my coven until they left me. Instead of wallowing in regret, I chose to embrace the memories. This was one of the incredibly rare occasions when I actually felt like Isaiah was right—I was still amazing, with or without my coven and my abilities. I would not let their absence kill me, and I would never be so desperate as to join the disgusting Virago to get my powers back.

I lifted Ike out of his high chair and set him on his feet. He ran across the room and dove onto the couch from three feet away. That child loved to ram into things. He bounced off and dove onto the couch again. He should have had a brother. We were always telling him, "Be careful, watch out," with Gwen and asking, "Do you see her sitting there?" for fear he'd just stomp over her.

Gwen was safely tucked in her bouncy chair on top of the table. When Ike bored of his couch diving, I'd let her lay on the family room floor. Gwen loved to bask in the morning sun that poured through the windows. I wiped the banana mush from her face and kissed her sweet nose. Gwen pulled herself up so she could watch Ike.

He screamed something I couldn't understand and flew across the room, knocking over a side chair in the process.

"Hey." I stepped into the doorway between the two rooms. "Be careful. You're going to break something. Like your arm."

He stared back at me with that sweet expression that could melt me into a yes, or no, or okay. Whatever he wanted.

I left my wrecking ball and turned my attention back to Gwen before she wailed her displeasure of being trapped for too long.

She was gone.

My heart stopped. Left my chest and disintegrated in the air. "Gwen!" I screamed.

Her lovely cooing sound rang through the kitchen. I twirled

around on my heels, searching every corner of the room for my daughter. The sound came again, and I followed it right to her seat on top of the table. She laughed her little baby laugh as I reached out and touched her invisible body, which was still strapped in the bouncy seat. *She was a witch.*

I didn't just watch her the rest of the day. I obsessed over her. Every single ounce of my focus was trapped on my daughter and her ability to disappear. I tried to "go" myself, but it never worked. I was solidly there in the house.

I didn't tell Isaiah about Gwen disappearing. He'd have reacted the same way he had when she'd thrown the book—as if I were insane and someone our children should be protected from. I swear that it was as if Helene had tortured him with witchcraft when they'd been together. She hadn't, though. Helene had been perfect, and while there had been obvious cracks in their relationship, Isaiah had memorialized their time together as flawless in his memory. I would never *be* her, and he would never *have* her.

That night, we lay next to each other in our bed. Our ankles practically touched, but he was farther away than he'd ever been before. The promise of witchcraft was dredging up memories neither of us could deal with. Not alone or together.

Light from the living room crept under the crack in our door. Ike was already climbing out of his crib, but he couldn't reach the switch yet. He must have been deviously creative to have turned the light on.

I slipped out of the covers and opened the door without making a sound. I wanted to see what my little one was up to without him knowing he'd been found. Ike's bedroom door was closed. So was the door to the nursery. There wasn't a sound from the house, not even the usual creaks from March's cruel wind.

"I'm sorry for not knocking," a man said, and my heart nearly stopped beating.

My head snapped in the direction in which the voice had come from, but there was no one there.

"Please don't be afraid."

I walked to the fireplace and took the poker in my hand. I swung it back and forth in front of me until the sound of it cutting through the air steadied me. "Who are you?"

"We haven't met. I'm a friend of Helene's."

There was no way for me to make sense of what he was saying. An invisible man, not a witch, who came to my house in the middle of the night and claimed to be a friend of my lost sister. "Helene who?"

There was only a hint of his dark laugh. "Oh, that's how you're playing it."

The exhilaration of the danger from my past life ran wild beneath my skin. The unknown and the invisible had been replaced decades ago by bottles and car seats. This man brought fear and deception and something was intoxicating about it, but I had no powers to protect myself. I would accept my trade of excitement for sippy cups if it meant keeping my family safe. "I want you to leave."

"I can't wait to go." He was next to me. His cool breath grazed my cheek and ignited the instinct to hurt him. I raised the poker between us. "I need to find out where Helene is."

He didn't want me. He was after Helene, and I'd never give her to him. "I don't know where she is. We haven't spoken in a while." A while . . . like, exactly four years, eight months, and six days. A while.

"Something changed today. For Helene. I lost track of her after she left the University of Vermont, but today was significant, and I don't know why." His voice softened, betraying the only reason he was in my house. This man was not interested in the same things as the Virago, but his intent was just as unclear.

"Why do you care?"

"I told you. We're friends."

His defiant tone reduced me to a teenager verbally sparring with the guy who sits in front of me in history. "Well, if you were friends, then you'd know what the big thing was."

He sighed heavily. "You have always been so difficult," he said as if he'd known me since I was a child. "If you had to guess where Helene is, where would it be?" His voice came from several feet away that time.

I knew her better than he knew her. He claimed to be her friend, but I'd been her sister. I constantly wondered where she was. On the way to the grocery store today, I'd decided Helene would be in Italy. As soon as she could, she would have gone there. Before Paris and Australia and Singapore, Helene would have to see Italy. It was the country that called to her the most.

I'd betrayed her once before, and I'd never do it again. "Brazil," I said. Even without her love, I'd be loyal. The way I should have been when we'd been eighteen.

"Italy, huh?" My attention whipped back toward the sound of his voice.

"How?"

"Not all of us have lost our gifts, Gisel."

I'd never known anyone who could read my thoughts unless I was directing them in the person's direction. The man occupying my living room was dangerous beyond any of my coven's understanding. "What did you say your name was again?"

"I didn't. Good night, Gisel." He taunted me with his knowledge of who I was.

The front door opened, and the night air rushed into the room. It pushed out a sweet smell that was reminiscent of the summer heat. I inhaled deeply the last molecules of it. It was honeysuckle.

The last sign of Gwen's birthright came on August sixteenth. She wasn't even a year old. I still had hope. Since March sixth, I'd kept the dream alive that with Gwen, my powers would return, but each attempt to move something or disappear was met with the harsh reality that I was no longer a witch. Every night before bed, I dutifully prayed to God the universe wouldn't forsake me the way my sisters had. I'd call out to them as soon as I shut my eyes.

Sloane, I know you can hear me, I would think, but I wasn't sure that she could.

Lovie, don't leave me.

And always for Helene, *I love you, and I'm sorry*, but the words were barely believable as Isaiah slept next to me. The sound of his peaceful slumber irritated me. I needed him. On some level, I loved him, but every day we were together, I let myself blame him to keep from hating myself.

On this particular August day, the heat was unbearable. Gwen and I were playing in the family room when she pulled herself up by the edge of the coffee table. She peeked up at me, waiting for her praise.

"Look at you," I said and kneeled down beside her. "What a big girl, standing all by yourself. Can you take a step?"

I reached out, beckoning her to let go of the table and step toward me. Gwen looked from my hands to the couch behind her. When she turned back to me, she giggled the sweet, baby giggle that always enchanted me. She raised her hands in the air and wobbled on her feet. She was going to take her first step. I should have videoed it, but I was too afraid to move, fearful she might fall over and bang her head on the table. With two hands spread wide at her sides, Gwen steadied herself and bounced a little on her feet. She smiled at me feeding my anticipation before she closed her eyes and flew to the seat of the couch.

My heart jumped in my chest. I rose to my feet and reveled in her delight at what she'd just accomplished. Gwen fell back onto her butt and kept giggling as she pulled her feet above her the way she used to before she could even sit up.

"Gwen, try it again. See if you can fly again," I begged, but Gwen's attention fell solidly on rolling around the soft cushions of the couch. When it was clear she was done flying, I found the index stuck to the inside of the kitchen cabinet.

November eighth—Gwen's Birthday

February twenty-third—threw a book

March sixth—disappeared

I added "August sixteenth—flew" and closed the cupboard door. I called the only person left in my life who would understand.

"Did you feel anything today?" I asked Mama, barely giving her a chance to say hello.

"Why?" Her voice was void of emotion, which lately was preferable to her irritation that did nothing but wear on me. She'd been hateful since her coven had died in the car accident decades ago and had only gotten worse after Dad passed away. I couldn't remember what it was like to have a mother and not this shell of anger I was tied to forever.

"Because your granddaughter flew this morning."

"Flew?" Finally, some emotion.

"Yes. She flew from the carpet all the way to the couch before my very eyes."

"Gisel—"

"Don't 'Gisel' me. This child is a witch. She has the power in her." I opened the cabinet door again. "I just have to figure out why her powers only showed on these dates." I reviewed them again, searching for the significance. Desperation rushed through me. Gwen's powers would slip again. I had to find a way to preserve them. It was her birthright. She was an Earth witch.

"Tell me the dates."

"February twenty-third, March sixth, and today. Plus, I was ready to ignite the day Gwen was born."

"They're their birthdays," my mother said as if she was sewing a hem and barely paused to answer.

"Whose?"

"Your wretched sisters' spawn. The new coven has been born. The one you and Gwen will never be a part of."

Of course. Lovie, Sloane, and Helene had all given birth within the same year as Gwen. The coven was born. It was there, waiting for my daughter to be a part of it. "What should I do?"

"I think you've done enough," she said, finally unleashing her bitterness on me.

"*I* have? Mother, if you'd had any love or even a sliver of restraint, I wouldn't be in this mess."

"Restraint? Like the type you exercised with your best friend's boyfriend." Her words cut through me. "You deserve this as much as they do." She was the worst mother in the world. I could argue the worst human being. Despise for her coated my brain with a renewed bitterness.

"You're a hateful woman."

I hung up on her. If she weren't my mother, I'd never speak to her again. In any other area of the world, people would applaud the decision, but this was Salem County, and we took care of our own. Even if we hated them.

Years passed, and on each of the dates, I watched for some sign that Gwen would carry on our family's legacy, but every year but her first, there'd been nothing. The dream died a little more with every day she grew older.

Until her junior year of high school. Something changed.

Many things.

I'd rather know darkness than mistake it for light.

Now . . .

I WALKED OUTSIDE TO FIND Ike stepping off the death-trap he'd begged us to let him buy. I'd said no to a motorcy-cle so many times that I'd forgotten all my logical reasons. Isaiah had finally convinced me to allow Ike the freedom, which I still regretted. It wasn't as if I'd ever had a favorite between my two children. I loved Ike and Gwen exactly the same. Ike just got left out of my thoughts sometimes because I was still consumed with the possibility of Gwen's powers. Isaiah acted as if he was in charge of making up for the slight in my attention.

I checked the time on my watch. "Did practice end early?"

"No," Ike said. He laughed. Making a joke out of my constant worry was the only way he knew how to respectfully handle me. It endeared me to him, but there wouldn't have to be a joke if he'd just drive a car like the rest of his classmates.

"Well, by my calculations you shouldn't be home for another four minutes. If you'd been doing the speed limit, that is." Ike needed to remember every rule I'd drummed into his head about the bike. The most important being his safety. "I'll take it away." I raised my eyebrows at him. The rules turned into fear of something happening to my firstborn. "Just because you're eighteen doesn't mean I can't."

"I'm fine. Very careful," Ike swore.

I clasped his face in my hands and stood on my tiptoes to kiss his forehead. I lowered halfway and trapped him in my glare. "Don't be that kid."

"What kid?" He was undaunted.

"The one who has the accident." Ike stepped out of my reach as if there was a chance of me dropping this subject. "The one who makes the *whole* town talk about how ridiculous it is that his mother let him get a motorcycle, and then he crashes it."

"Are you more worried about me having an accident, or you being wrong about something?"

My greatest fear slid down my back. "I won't go on without you," I said and again questioned how I could have ever let him get that awful bike.

"I'm fine," Ike said. "I promise I'll be careful. I know you're putting a lot of trust in me."

"Why can't you just drive a car?"

He laughed at me the same way he always did. "I like flying."

"I hear you." The depth of my understanding was lost to Ike.

I dropped the topic for the night. If I kept it up, he was going to start avoiding me, and the only thing less tolerable than my son riding a motorcycle was him ignoring me. I handed Ike a mum and motioned to the side yard for him to carry it out. I grabbed a mixed orange and red one and followed him to the flowerbed. I wanted to keep him talking and for him to tell me every detail of his day the way he used to when I picked him up from the Preschool Academy. Back then, it was Miss Kelly this, and Miss Kathy that. Since he no longer needed help into the car seat, I got nothing. "Gwen said homecoming's in a few weeks."

Ike rolled his eyes. He and his sister were closer in age than in mindsets. "I bet she did."

"Any thoughts on a date?" He closed his eyes and shook his head at my question, which only fueled my tenacity. If he thought he could outlast me, he was in for a long life. He should talk to his father about it. "What about that nice girl we saw at the custard stand last weekend?"

"Maybe." His answer was quick and noncommittal. On to the next one.

"What was her name?" I wanted him to fall in love . . . but only for a little while. It had to end in a mutually mature way that left him unscarred. Was that too much for a mother to ask for?

"Her name is Grace, and I don't think it's going to work out."

I packed in the soil around the base of the mum and faced my beautiful son. "Why? You seemed to like her just fine at the end of the summer."

"Things have changed."

"Sure they have." Nothing ever changes in this town. I left Ike by the flowerbed and searched through the oars, bikes, and snow shovels littering the garage to find my favorite trowel.

When I stepped out of the garage, Ike was leaning on one hand on the corner of the house. He was hunched over as if whispering to someone, but when I walked past him, I could see there was no one there.

"Are you coming in?" Something about his stance and the silence of the evening wanted both of us inside with the doors shut. I could feel a presence other than my son, but I had no idea what it was. The tiny hairs on my arms rose. I tilted my head to take in the breeze before asking, "What are you doing?"

"I thought I felt someone," Ike said.

I stopped breathing. "Felt?" My chest tightened at the possibilities of who was with us in our yard.

Ike shook his head, taking a step toward me. "Saw something." His eyes lingered on the corner of the house.

I walked backward into the garage, making sure Ike was following me. It seemed a cool breeze flowed behind us and through the door. It was a stifling realization that followed Ike's stare down the side of our home and strummed my heartbeat in my chest. We weren't alone.

"What's wrong with you?" Isaiah asked with the patience of a man whose wife exhausted him. Ike walked past us without a word. He was old enough to sense the coming conversation.

"Nothing." I washed my hands in the kitchen sink.

Isaiah leaned on the counter next to the sink and crossed his arms at his chest. "Gisel, what's wrong?" His tone made me sick.

I wanted to scream at him, "What's wrong?" My husband knew exactly the moments in time that haunted me because he was with me when they'd been set into motion. He'd dragged me down to the center of hell with him. "You've ruined my life."

He stood and squared his jaw. "I ruined your life?" He didn't even bother to placate me anymore. If I still had the use of my powers, I'd have lodged something in his throat. *A bottle cap, perhaps.* "You're turning into your mother." *Or maybe an ax.*

"Shut up, Isaiah." She was a topic we rarely spoke of. My mother, my coven, my sisters, my birthright, my powers . . . my misery. She may have been responsible for most of this, but she was still my mother. It was bad enough I had to deal with her because of the obligation bestowed upon a daughter. I didn't have to hear Isaiah's thoughts on our likeness as well.

"The truth hurts."

I dried my hands and threw the towel in his face. "You're a pathetic excuse for a man."

"And you're an angry, bitter woman." He needed a release. We hadn't been together in weeks, and it always left Isaiah quick to reduce me to the lowest version of myself in his mind. I'd have to find a way to stand him touching me long enough to reset the counter on the days until he hated me again. I'd made my bed. It was time to lay in it.

I leaned in close to him and lowered my voice. "And I'm your wife," I said, reminding him I was as good as it was going to get for him. Isaiah could have left. If he weren't afraid of my mother's wrath, he probably would have already, but he was as weak as he'd been decades ago. I was no better. I could have left just as easily as he could have.

Yet, there I still was.

Hours later, I found him out back sitting by the fire. He held a large glass filled with ice and brown liquid. It was his drink when he was trying to forget. Rum and Coke. He'd drown in it if it meant he could erase his memory.

I sat in the chair next to him and let the fire warm my toes. Tomorrow he'd go to work, and then we'd go to the football game together. It would be a busy day filled with other people instead of each other. We wouldn't even sit together at the game. I'd known Isaiah so long that it wasn't necessary to sit by his side, not that I wanted to.

We'd also been together long enough that I usually could tell what he was thinking from fifty yards away, but as he stared into the flames, I didn't know what was in his head. I wasn't sure when this had become our marriage. As I thought about it, I realized I wasn't even sure what I'd imagined our marriage to be. I'd just moved forward with it and walked down the aisle. I hadn't let myself think of what I wanted beyond my coven and my powers back.

I sipped my wine. I could walk over to him, cuddle in next to him, and hold his hand, or I could sit right here and ignore him the way he ignored me.

With silence came the memories, and those I could not tolerate. "Maybe we should entertain more?" He looked my way, but not at me. "We've got the new kitchen and this great patio. We should have some people over. It's not like the kids want to hang out with us anymore." God forbid. Ike couldn't get out of the house fast enough, and Gwen was becoming the same way.

"Whatever you want," he answered in that nonchalant way that always managed to piss me off. He knew I was trying here, and his lack of interest was displayed on purpose, but I was unfazed.

"Maybe Tommy and Angie. I haven't seen them in weeks."

"Tommy was here yesterday. He borrowed the log splitter."

"Oh." I must have missed him.

Isaiah sighed and finally made eye contact with me. The rum was taking effect. A small smile broke through his melancholy. He was incapable of holding a grudge. On that we differed. "I'm sorry for saying you're like your mother," he said.

I'm sorry for wanting to lodge something in your throat and watch you gasp for air as you died at my feet. "Apology accepted," is what I actually offered.

My husband laughed and returned his focus to the fire.

All this school spirit is exhausting me.

I WAS BARELY PAYING ATTENTION to the game. Trish was waving at me. She couldn't wait to tell me the latest, I was sure. Project Graduation, and the fifty-fifty sales to raise money for it, was the current conversation I was dragged into on the sideline with the woman I'd avoided conversations with the past four years. Trish would have to be patient.

I heard the helmets connect and looked up in time to see Ike hit the ground and roll onto his back. Everyone around me shouted and booed, but all I could take in was my son. He didn't move. Players, coaches, and other adults surrounded him. The muscles in my arms began to vibrate and shake. I pulled my wrists close to my body to steady them. I needed to listen and see.

"Is that Ike?" the woman droning on and on about homecoming asked. My stomach turned in waves that reached my throat. "Oh my God. It is, Gisel."

I knew it was him. He was my son. I could feel his pain from a thousand miles away. I didn't need this overly organized blowhard telling me. I rushed toward the fence.

"Wait!" Isaiah yelled. I turned back to find him just standing around as if it were someone else's child on the ground. He was useless. If I still had my powers, I'd have set him on fire and put him out of his misery.

"I will not wait." A surge of power infiltrated my body. I inhaled deeply until my breath caught. The sight of the girl standing on the fence stole my attention. She was a witch. I inhaled again as a renewed energy coursed through me. The girl clutched the fence as if it were the only thing holding her up.

"They'll take care of him." Isaiah grabbed my arm, and I wanted to tear it off my body and beat him with it, but there was no time. I yanked it away and continued to my son.

No one else tried to stop me, and seconds later, I kneeled near my son's head. His helmet was still on. Words were being said. His eyes were closed. Air rushed at me as harsh as a scream. It came from the fence in waves of commands.

I glared at the girl on the fence again—sure it was coming from her.

The paramedics came on the field, but nothing would register. I couldn't make out directions or assessments until my son opened his eyes. The stadium was completely silent, and I let my mind follow.

I stayed on the ground until Ike was moved onto the stretcher. Isaiah should have been there to help me up. A new gust blew at me, and I rose to my feet, gaining strength from it. Even without my powers, I still didn't need a man.

"We're going to Salem," I called out as I followed the paramedics.

"We'll follow you," Isaiah yelled back.

I let the paramedics do their job. We were jammed in their mobile hospital with my son, who still hadn't opened his eyes. How

long had it been? I was sweating. There wasn't enough air in the
ambulance to keep us all alive. I needed Ike to say something in
order to be able to breathe.

The woman working near Ike's head looked up, and her hair
blew back off her face. The breeze was absent from the rest of the
ambulance. I tilted my head and thought I heard someone yelling
for Ike to wake up. It was a frantic and desperate plea, and for a
moment, I thought it had come from my mouth.

Ike's eyes opened with anticipation. His gaze darted around the
ambulance as if looking for the person who'd just slapped him.

"Ike, I'm right here," I said and rubbed his arm. My fingers
barely touched his skin, but I moved them up and down and back
and forth until the expression on his face softened and he calmed.
"You're okay." I leaned out the back door and searched the crowd
for Gwen and Isaiah. They were running toward his truck. "He's
awake," I yelled, and the ambulance door was closed.

Ike's focus rested on the roof without any indication he'd heard
me.

"That's good," the paramedic said. "Keep talking to him."

"Ike, it's Mom. I love you." The paramedic on the other side of
my son was in constant motion. She spoke to the driver. None of
the sentences registered past the sight of Ike beside me. "Ike. You're
going to be fine. You're the strongest guy I know." I was running
out of things to say because I wasn't going to tell him he'd be back
on the field in no time, and none of it seemed to matter. He was
lost somewhere inside his head. My son wasn't paying any attention
to me. "Ike!" I sharpened my tone.

"Mom, I hear you," he finally answered without trying to look
my way. "It's okay," he said and exhaled roughly over the collar
around his neck.

I kept rubbing his arm and telling him how much I loved him
until we pulled into the emergency room entrance at the Salem

County Memorial Hospital. They took him from me there. Even if I'd had my powers, I would have had to let him go, but separating him from my sight was nearly impossible. He took a part of me behind the door, leaving me standing in the waiting room without a heartbeat. There was nothing left alive inside my body. Ike had it all with him.

When Isaiah and Gwen rushed in, I was still standing alone in the center of the rows of chairs. My husband pulled me into his arms and held me tight against his chest. The wool collar of his coat smelled like the fire we'd lit out back the night before. The one we'd sat next to and had nothing to say to each other.

"I'm here," he said, and tears broke through my resentment of him. It was always Isaiah who was still there. I cried into the strength of his shoulders and the heaviness of his arms. "It's okay. I'm here."

I closed my eyes and let myself be held up by my husband. He'd done it so many times over the years that I'd forgotten to be grateful. "Thank you," I said.

Isaiah squeezed my shoulders before walking me over to the chairs next to Gwen and helping me to sit. The three of us waited to hear any news about the boy we loved more than ourselves. When the minutes turned into an hour, Isaiah took my hand in his and held it on his lap. One silent tear slipped down my cheek. I wiped it away before Gwen could see it.

The sliding door to the examination area opened again. I'd memorized the sound within minutes of arriving. The footsteps traveled toward us, and mercifully a woman in a white coat stood in front of us.

"Mr. and Mrs. Kennedy?"

"Yes."

"He's okay."

I inhaled, and my body finally let the air fully reach my lungs. I'd been existing in shallow waters until I knew Ike was all right.

"You can come back and see him now."

Seeing him wasn't enough. I wanted to hold him and talk to him and make him tell me every little thing that had happened to him since we'd been separated. "Can we take him home?"

"I'm going to recommend he stay the night," the doctor said and led us through the sliding door. "He's responsive. The tests have come back fine . . ."

"But?" Isaiah asked. We all stopped moving.

"But there are moments where he seems to be unaware of his surroundings. I don't think it's serious, just a delay in response. As if he's somewhere else in his mind." The image of Ike staring at the ceiling of the ambulance came back to me. "He's able to answer questions, knows where he is. I think it might be exhaustion, but we want to keep an eye on him."

Every word she said was released from my mind at the sight of my son on the gurney. He'd been changed into a hospital gown. A paper bag held his uniform in the chair next to him and another larger bag held his game pads and helmet. His eyes were so light they resembled mine more than his father's. When he saw me, he laughed as if he could read my mind and the results of my examination were absurd.

"I'm fine," he said and shook his head.

"We know you are." Isaiah smoothed the hair off Ike's face as he spoke. "A little bump isn't going to get the best of you."

"A little bump," Gwen said and squeezed Ike's toes the way he'd hated his entire life.

"I'll throw you in the lake as soon as I get out of here."

"I'm going home to take a ride on your bike." She tilted her head a little at the tail end of her taunt.

"I'll break both your legs."

"Okay," I said and took Ike's hand in mine. "It sounds like you're feeling better."

"At least good enough to kill his little sister," Isaiah added. He took in both his children and smiled. He'd always wanted to be a dad. He used to talk about it in high school. Even back when he was with—

"We're going to move him," a nurse said as she opened the curtain surrounding Ike's area.

I wasn't more than ten inches from him the entire way to room three sixty-five B. Isaiah gave me the look. He was preparing me for our departure, but if Ike even so much as hesitated when we said goodbye, I was going to stand right next to him until daylight came and I could take him home with me.

The nurse came in to make sure he was settled. Ike threw a smile my way. It was the same one he'd used the first time he'd taken off on that horrible motorcycle. It was the one he reserved for his mom when she was losing her mind. I kissed his forehead. "I love you," I said and hoped he realized the words didn't begin to describe how I felt about him.

Isaiah dropped his jeans to the floor, stepped out of them, and threw them over the chair in the corner of our bedroom.

"Once, when I was flying with Sloane over the Delaware River into Wilmington, the Virago tried to drown us," I said. Isaiah stopped changing his clothes. His expression gave away nothing of what he might be thinking. "They pushed us down until we were screaming for help inside our heads." I crossed my arms over my chest to protect me from the memories. Terror clenched my teeth and dried my throat. It wasn't the same fear I'd had that day, but the tiny tremors that always came when I thought of that day toyed with my muscles in my husband's sight. "The weight pressed against me until my face touched the water. I thought I was going to die." Isaiah's eyes bore into mine with nothing but compassion.

"And that wasn't anywhere near as scary as tonight was."

"I know." He walked over and hugged me again. My husband kissed the top of my head and squeezed my shoulders. "I know how much you love him, Gisel."

An enormously inconceivable reality came to me. "How do people function when their children are hurt . . . or worse?"

"They lean on the people who love them." He raised my chin until I was looking into the eyes that had stared at me when I'd walked down the aisle to him and when he'd carried me over the threshold of this house and when I'd delivered both our babies.

I stood on my tiptoes and kissed my husband with a recognition that had been lost over the years. The stress of the night, the months—years—of loneliness edged forward until he threw me onto our bed and climbed in after. Isaiah took from me what I'd denied us both for too long. I'd replaced any need for my husband with disdain. He would change that. I closed my eyes and savored the weight of him on top of me.

After we'd caught our breath and let go of the final exhale, Isaiah rolled over and turned off the light on his side of the bed. I stayed facing him in the glimmer from the moon. Isaiah stared at the ceiling until he finally asked, "How did you get out of the water?"

"What water?"

"The Delaware. How did you escape the Virago?"

"Helene came and saved me," I said. I rolled over and returned to the reality of my life.

I lay on my back, watched the moonlight on the ceiling, and listened. He fell asleep within minutes of closing his eyes. I wasn't as lucky. Memories of my sisters haunted me until the image of the girl on the fence replaced them in my mind. Without Ike lying on the field, I could properly consider her. She'd looked to be about Gwen's age, standing next to her, but nothing stood out about her except the power she'd ignited within me. That, and the moment on the field when I'd felt as if she was piercing me with her thoughts. Something had drawn me to look at her. To see her more closely, because I'd suddenly felt as if I'd wandered into her line of fire. Or thought. I shook my head and closed my eyes. This was crazy. I'd been upset about Ike. I needed to sleep. It was the only thing that healed me from the past.

"Helene," Isaiah said. The word was almost a moan. I couldn't tell if he was in pain or somewhere else in his mind. It wasn't the first time he'd said her name in his sleep. I was again thankful I never dreamed. The memories tortured me enough when I was awake.

Nothing changes around here.
We used to drink in a bunch of fields, too.

THIS WAS SALEM COUNTY. FINDING out the name of the girl at the football game should take all of about five minutes on the phone with anyone in this town. If I didn't know who she was, it was a sure bet everyone else was talking about her.

I chose not to make any phone calls and instead drove to the school with a bagged lunch in my passenger seat. It didn't matter that both my kids had brought lunch to school. It was nothing more than an excuse to get inside and chat up the receptionist. No matter how many times I walked through the front doors of the building, the same old feelings of what it was like to be sixteen flooded back. I couldn't shake them and I didn't want to.

I opened the door and walked up the front steps to find Denny Taylor sitting at a table with a clipboard in front of him.

"Hey, Gisel."

"Hi, Denny. I heard you were working security."

"I am. What are you doing here? You're a little old for Spanish."

"Says you." I turned toward the office.

"Hold up." I stopped and twirled on my heel. "I can take care of whatever you need." He tipped his head toward the lunch in my hands. "Ike or Gwen forget their lunch?"

"Ike."

"You can leave it here, and I'll get it to him." This new security was stupid. It was my school, too. I should be able to walk into it whenever I pleased.

"Actually, I wanted to talk to Trish. Does she still work in the office?"

"Oh, you'll know when she leaves. The building will fall to the ground."

Denny and I laughed. "She always did have it all together." We shook our heads until I stepped toward the office, and Denny let me go.

Trish was sitting at her desk behind the counter just waiting to tell me everything she'd learned since the last time I'd seen her. "Hey, girl," she said as I opened the door. "What are you doing here?"

"Ike forgot his lunch." I held up the bag.

"I'll let him know." Trish wasn't herself. Gone was the animated response and the too-loud voice. I just stood there smiling at her until she said, "Did you hear Dr. Wilson is cheating on his wife?"

"No." I hadn't. No one would have even imagined it. He was a family man. Apparently, he preferred more than one family.

Trish lowered her voice. "With some drug rep from Delaware."

"Oh." It was a shame, but I didn't care.

"Men are such pigs." She tilted her head to the side. "But you know all about that."

I was solid. Not even a flinch. This town would never let history die.

Trish tilted her head and seemed to really be examining me, not just disseminating information as usual. I braced myself for the results of her assessment. "Have you seen them since they came back?" she asked.

I kept staring straight ahead at Trish, but I couldn't breathe. There was no question who she meant. The entire world was suddenly and hopefully different from how it had been when I'd woken that morning. I let out enough air to keep me on my feet. "No," I managed to say. Had the word been more than one syllable, I might have faltered.

Trish leaned back, giving me a few more inches to work with. "Well, they look exactly the same. Gorgeous." She waved her hand at me. "All of you were always so pretty."

"Trish, have you seen the agenda for tomorrow night's board meeting? I printed it to this printer." I smiled at Principal Jeffries. He wasn't from Woodstown. For some reason, I was extra nice to him because of it. "Oh, hello, Mrs. Kennedy. Signing someone out?"

"No. Just dropping off a lunch." I set the bag on the counter and pushed it toward Trish. He needed to go back into his office. I had more questions. How long had they been back? Were any of them with their husbands? Where were they staying? Principal Jeffries continued to smile until I said, "I'll see you guys later."

"Have a nice day," they both replied at the same time, and the uniformity was awkward, or maybe it was my hesitance to walk away.

I exited the office just as the bell rang and waited against the wall until Ike passed by.

"Ike," I said.

He stopped and stared at me. His black hair was growing out and a curl hit perfectly on his forehead. It was impossible to imagine he, and every other boy in this building, was in danger from a curse cast years before he was even born. Ike stepped across the crowded hall, forcing the other students to avoid him. "What are you doing here?"

"I brought your lunch." I wanted to grab him and Gwen and take them out of the school. The way the girl had stared at my son from the sideline when he was hurt kept beating against the inside of my head. There was already a connection.

"I told you I was buying." He studied my face.

"Ike," his friend, Paul, called. Ike waved toward him, and then his gaze followed the girl from the fence as she walked down the hall.

Like a bullet shot into the center of my chest, energy coursed through me, and I knew. I searched her face for her mother's identity. She didn't resemble Lovie, Sloane, or Helene, but there was something about her. She was part of me. I was sure of it.

"Can you walk me out? I need to talk to you," I said.

"I'll be late."

"I don't care." I pulled his elbow, urging him toward the front door. Once outside, I turned on him and grabbed my burly son by both arms. "There's a new girl in Gwen's class this year?"

Ike's face scrunched in confusion the same way it did when he was a toddler. "Yeah. A few."

My eyebrows rose. "The one with long brown hair and green eyes. What's her name?"

"Ever?"

I inhaled sharply. She was Helene's. Only Helene would choose the name Ever. "What's her last name?"

"Um." Again he studied my face. "I think Ayars."

"Okay. You are not to see her. Like, do not hang out with her, spend time with her, talk to her . . . none of it."

"Mom. You sound like a crazy person."

"Do you hear me?" My voice was sharp and on the edge of yelling.

"Yeah. I barely know her. What is the big deal?"

I was losing my grip. Trish had stolen it when she'd said they were home, and I couldn't get it back. How long would they stay? Were they ever planning on seeing me? I refocused on my beautiful son. "Just stay away from all of them. As far as you possibly can."

The bell rang. "I have to go," Ike said. He walked up the front stairs and glanced back over his shoulder at his lunatic mother as he opened the front door.

I smiled weakly at him. It was all I had.

I flew home. Not literally. The same bitter realization that always hit me when I used that phrase nearly buried me.

I sat at the computer in the office nook just off the kitchen. When we'd remodeled, Isaiah had insisted we needed a place for the kids to do their homework or research, but they both had laptops. Isaiah and I were the only people who used the area. I resisted the urge to type "Helene Ayars," and instead brought up the search history for the computer. Before I looked for her, I wanted to know if Isaiah had.

The idea that he'd seen her, run into her, or even met with her without my having a clue was absurd. He couldn't keep something like that from me. Although, that was exactly what I was planning to do to him. Until I had a handle on what their return meant, Isaiah need not be involved. He had a history of ruining everything, and he hadn't lost nearly as much as I had. There was nothing of interest in the search data. When Isaiah went to sleep, I'd search for the same information on his phone.

I leaned back and looked through the kitchen and out into the backyard, confirming it was empty and that I was alone. Each letter of her name I typed with the same precision as if I were bringing her to life in front of me. There was very little to find. An obituary for Owen Ayars six years ago was the first thing I clicked on.

Owen joined the United States Marine Corp. He graduated boot camp from Parris Island, South Carolina, which began a six-year career that led him to serve in multiple locations including Okinawa, Japan, 29 Palms,

*California, Camp Lejeune, North Carolina, Kuwait, and Korea. He cou-
rageously fought in both Iraq and Afghanistan.*

I sat back and stared at the screen. I closed my eyes and fought back the guilt that plagued me every minute of the day.

Owen was a loving and devoted husband to his wife, Helene (Paulsen), and was survived by his daughter, Ever Ayars.

"What are you doing back here?" my mother asked me, appearing out of nowhere.

She startled me. "Mama, how did you get here?"

"I flew," she said with complete disdain for my thinking she hadn't.

"You cannot still be flying. You can barely see, and your heart . . ."

"If I die flying, I'll be the happiest I've ever been."

"And what happens when your body falls from the sky directly onto the roof of a car? How will I explain that?"

"That's not my problem." A coughing fit overtook her. She leaned against the desk and held on until the color returned to her face. Her eyes fell to the computer screen. She leaned over and squinted to read the words.

"Come sit down. I'll get you some tea."

"Helene Ayars." Of course, that would be the one thing she would actually see clearly. "That's her name now?"

"Yes. I think so." I walked into the kitchen, leaving her reading the obituary of Helene's deceased husband.

"You're better off without her."

The statement was ridiculous. I could barely breathe without them. "You did this, Mama. You should have never cursed them."

"Poppycock. They deserved it. They broke the coven."

"*I* broke it. I did it. You're punishing them for something that I did."

"No matter what you did . . ." She followed me into the kitchen. I was tired of saying the same old thing to her. "*They* left you here powerless. That's not what a coven does. It's for a lifetime."

"How about your coven, Mama? How are you honoring them?"

She leaned on the counter as if standing was an effort. "I'm beginning to think it was never worth fighting for."

"Well, you're wrong, and if you didn't still have your powers, that'd be a lot easier for you to see."

"You should forget they exist."

I let her go on. I wasn't going to tell her that my coven had returned to Auburn. Like Isaiah, my mother had done enough to ruin all of our lives.

From that day forward, there was a great deal to watch. I kept one eye on Isaiah. Every mention of the weather chilling, homecoming, the football games, or anything that might bring back a memory of Helene was scrutinized like never before. If he knew she was in town, I wanted to know how.

I also watched Ike, because the way he looked at Ever that day in the hallway was unmistakable. I'd seen his father stare at the girl's mother the same way for years. There was no denying that type of attraction. If left unchecked, it'd be weeks if not days until they united, and my son anywhere near Helene's daughter was out of the question.

Gwen threatened to steal my attention from all of it. She was glowing. I inhaled deeply, feeding off her power every time she entered the room.

"Can you turn on the light by the sink?" I'd ask with my head turned. Without hearing any movement behind me, the light turned on, and I knew she'd done it with her mind.

"Mom. Did you ever feel like you were supposed to be somewhere else? Someone else?" she asked. There was fear in her eyes, and it was breaking my heart. This was her birthright.

"Yes. Sometimes, the idea almost cripples me." Gwen nodded. Her concerns were eased by my understanding. "Gwen, you can talk to me about anything. No matter how crazy it sounds."

"I know." She spoke too quickly. She wasn't going to divulge anything. I wasn't sure if I should push or not.

"Are you looking forward to your party?"

"Yes."

"How many people are we up to?"

"Forty-one." She said the number with hesitation. Her father had told her twenty. In my head, I'd capped the invites at fifty, but really, I only cared about three.

"I heard there are some new girls in your class."

Gwen stopped moving about the kitchen and dropped the mail onto the counter in front of her. "There are. Three." This was the moment I should infiltrate. Gwen would talk to me if I told her what I already knew. "From Auburn," she added. But the mention of the town—*my* town—rendered me speechless.

She slipped me a short smile and walked out of the room. A few bumps and colliding sounds came from behind her door. She was moving things and returning them to their places. Gwen's powers were gaining strength. Her coven was intact. I just didn't think she knew it yet.

❦

The morning of Gwen's birthday party, Mama fell when she was getting out of bed. She wasn't badly injured, but I still brought her to our house to spend the night. I borrowed our neighbor's small travel wheelchair, and to my utter surprise, Mama sat in it when I opened it for her. Her compliance was a clear indication she was hurting far worse than I originally thought.

When I had her settled in front of the television with a cup of tea, Isaiah asked, "This is temporary, right?"

I assured him it was just as the first guest arrived for the party. My mother watched out the front window as more kids were dropped off. Their laughter and well wishes carried through the frigid November air and into the warm room on the front of our house. Ike, who had been silent all afternoon, had shown up with a cut hand and anger oozing from his pores. Isaiah had forced me to give him space, but he didn't know that with space came the possibility of Ike seeing Ever Ayars, and *that* was completely out of the question.

"I should have killed them. Awful rule, a witch not being able to kill another witch."

My heart was frozen to the walls of my chest. The hatred in my mother's eyes bore through the window and beyond to the three girls standing in the driveway with Gwen. They were laughing and hugging. "Carrying on as if they belong together when their mothers and grandmothers ripped us all apart." Ever looked nothing like Helene, but the other two were their mothers. From the strawberry-blond hair to the thick dark tresses of the short one. The four of them together were practically sparkling. There was a closeness between them I hadn't felt in twenty years. "Your idiot husband has survived his marriage by not noticing the obvious, but you know. You can see them as well as I can."

"Mama, you're crazy. They're a bunch of young girls." Ever wished Gwen a happy birthday, and Gwen nodded as if in response to a wordless conversation. The sight of the four of them together was captivating but dangerous with my mother nearby. I wheeled her around until she faced the fireplace.

"The tall one is Helene's."

"Mama. She looks nothing like Helene."

"Maybe not her hair or her eye color, but she stands just like her, and her voice is her grandmother's. That, I'll never forget." There was a moment of sadness from my mother. She'd lost so much, too. She was as alone as I was, but we couldn't support each other. "They should have never come back."

The heat rose up the back of my neck. I never should have slept with Isaiah. Helene, Sloane, and Lovie should have let me explain. My mother never should have hexed them. They should have never left. We all should have done something differently. "You sound insane."

"And you are clueless if you don't see they're a coven."

"As they should be." I straightened my back and faced my horrid mother.

"It's all dead. Because of their mother's—"

Gwen walked into the room. Mama started to finish her sentence, but I stopped her with, "That's enough." Gwen looked from her mimi to me. "How's it going?" I asked with a lightness to my voice that sounded as fake as it was.

"We need more drinks."

"I'll send your father and brother out with some." I listened to the silent rooms in our house. "Where are they?"

"I don't know where Dad is, but Ike's down by the lake."

"By himself?" My chest tightened again. He needed to find a girlfriend other than Helene's daughter.

"Yeah," Gwen said and stepped out of the house onto the side patio.

"You need to get your house in order," my mother said as soon as the door slid shut behind my daughter.

"What are you talking about?" I'd let her believe I was clueless to keep her in the dark.

"Starting with your son."

I watched them. Ike was my main concern. I tried not to let him out of my sight, but even though he was huge and constantly impacting the world, he shunned the spotlight. He mixed in with the other teenagers spread out across my back lawn. The more pressing obstacle was the energy pouring off my daughter's coven. I wanted to sink into them every time they came near me. To sit down and ask them every question about their mothers that had popped into my head since they'd left me alone in Auburn.

Are your mothers happy? Did they tell you about Auburn? Do they ever mention me?

I wanted to know if Lovie and Sloane's husbands were still alive.

My head lowered with the shame of my past. I'd need to visit Trish again to find out the information. Unless Gwen already knew.

Or Ike . . .

I wouldn't think about that. I grabbed my camera off the kitchen counter and stepped outside into the garage. Two girls were locked in an ominous conversation by the table where the cake sat, cut, and plated. The tall one mentioned Ike before the other girl shushed her and smiled at me. I breezed past them and began taking candid photos of the crowd around the bonfire. I'd make a scrapbook for Gwen of her seventeenth birthday. I'd spent mine with the mothers of the girls who now surrounded her.

They were laughing without a care in the world. I imagined I'd been the same twenty years ago.

"Ruby, you cannot say that," the dark-haired one said. I snapped a photo and hid my laughter behind the camera. Sloane had named her daughter Ruby. Sloane would have simultaneously hated and loved the name. She hadn't changed a bit. Still fighting the predictable with the unexpected and loving them both.

Gwen faced them and told a story with her hands held high in the air, waving as if she were a theatrical act. Ever stood between the others. She was the middle the same way her mother had always been. I took the opportunity to take a picture of just the three of them. Ruby's gaze shifted from Gwen to my lens. She scrutinized my photography rather than smiling, obviously as cunning as her mother.

I nonchalantly turned, panning the crowd for another subject until Isaiah came into view. He was lost in thought, leaning against the corner of the house and watching the girls who I had my back to. My husband was captivated by the daughter of his last love. Isaiah's mouth hung open a little. He clutched the side of the house as if he couldn't breathe and hold himself up at the same time.

I didn't hate him. Pity was all I felt for my husband. Except on the days I let the guilt in, then I felt responsible that both of us were so alone and still with each other. A slight fear emerged of what he'd do now that he knew they were back. If he could take his eyes off Ever for a second, he'd notice Sloane and Lovie were in town, too. He'd put together all the pieces until he realized I'd been right Gwen's entire life. Her coven had been born the same year she'd come to us, and it wasn't going to be ignored.

The girls were the first to say goodbye. Ever never even looked back at Ike. He seemed equally as uninterested as he got on his bike and was "free" of his little sister's party and able to go wherever senior boys were hanging out these days. I assumed it was in the woods or a field somewhere. Probably sneaking cigarettes in a woodshop on Stewart Road.

I settled into the routine motions of cleaning up as Gwen said goodbye to all her guests, even the ones whose rides forgot to pick them up. Gwen was patient and kind as she entertained them in our garage while they waited. I was wrapping the last of the leftover cake when Isaiah came into the kitchen and stood beside me at the counter.

"When were you going to tell me?" His voice buoyed on his twenty-year-old hatred. My hands stopped moving. My emotions all mixed together. Dealing with Isaiah tonight was too much to ask of my sanity.

"What?"

"What." He repeated my ridiculous response. His fingers formed tight fists and turned white with aggression.

"Shh—" I said as Gwen walked into the kitchen.

"They're finally gone." The thick air swirling between her father and I couldn't be split with her lightness. "What's going on?" she asked, turning from her father to me and back again.

"Nothing." Isaiah just stood there, wallowing in his anger. "Did you have fun?"

Gwen never took her eyes off him as she answered, "Yes."

"It looked like you had some new friends here tonight," he probed.

"Yes. From Aubu—"

"You can tell us all about them in the morning. It's late, and you look exhausted," I said before Gwen could continue. "Off to bed, birthday girl."

With a guarded smile, Gwen said, "Good night." She thanked us both and kissed us on the cheeks before she left the room.

Isaiah and I listened to her brushing her teeth in the bathroom, the light switch turning off, and finally her bedroom door shutting before he said, "You know *what*, Gisel. When were you going to tell me they're back?"

I straightened and placed the cake on the top shelf of the refrigerator. "I don't know what you mean." I wasn't referring to Lovie, Sloane, and Helene. More to the idea that it was my job to inform Isaiah of their whereabouts.

He turned around, crossed his arms in front of him, and leaned back on the counter while he watched me move about the kitchen. "Did you honestly think there was a chance I wouldn't find out?" He was indignant. "With them all together in my house?" Completely aggrieved.

"What is it that you *think* you know?" His stare bore into me until the defensive was no longer a safe position. "You're an idiot." Isaiah shook his head while his lips pursed in disgust. "What makes you think it's them?"

Bitter satisfaction replaced the anger on his face. I braced myself for his retaliation. Over the years, we'd run out of ways to hurt each other, but with my coven's return came old ammunition. "Because she turned her head toward me and smiled, and the shape of her chin, the curve of her lips . . . the resemblance to Helene almost knocked me to the ground. She doesn't look like her, but she's hers."

I turned toward the two liter bottles of soda floating in the bucket near the sink. I exhaled and let my shoulders drop. He wasn't nearly as blind as Mama had claimed. At least not when it came to Helene. When I didn't offer him any explanation or answer, Isaiah stormed out of the house, letting the screen door slam behind him.

Only a broken heart could cause destruction like this.

IT WAS JUST LITTLE THINGS at first—the movement of inanimate objects with no one near them, but with Gwen always in the room. She never tired of turning lights on and off when I was around to see, but twice I overheard her in the bathroom saying, "Now disappear." I assumed she was standing in front of the mirror "going" the way I used to be able to. I tapped my fingertips against my thumb. Still nothing.

"You both have to clean your rooms before you leave this house."

"We're going to be late," Ike said. He had more time since he rode that horrible motorcycle to school. Gwen had to be at the end of the road in twelve minutes to catch the bus.

I made my way down the hall to their bedrooms in time to find Gwen surveying her pristine space with a satisfied look on her face. Ike followed me through her door and took in every inch of her now-clean room. He and Gwen shared a knowing look, and then he shrugged and walked out. *He knows.*

I sat at the kitchen table and let the panic set in as first Gwen, and then Ike, left the house. I turned my cup of coffee around until the Cowtown Rodeo logo faced me. Air ran up the back of my neck and swirled around my face. I opened my mouth to inhale the freshness. It powered down to my lungs. My eyes closed, and my head fell back as the newness infected me. When I opened them, I stared at the faucet until the handle tilted back and water flowed. My breath caught. My powers were returning. I rubbed my palms together, searching for the exquisite energy, but there was none. Only a hint of honeysuckle in the air that immediately put me on edge.

The water turned off, and he said, "Hello, Gisel," as if speaking to me was the most boring part of his day.

"Who *are* you?" I was sick of the invisible man's visits, and since I was regaining my powers, I'd eventually be able to show him exactly how tired of him I was.

"Simmer down," he said, reminding me he could read my mind, which was the *most* infuriating thing about him.

"What do you want? And why can't you be a normal person and let me see you?"

"Who says you get to decide what's normal?"

I rolled my eyes. "I'm busy looking at the wall, so if you're done, you can leave."

He sighed, and the exhaled air swept across my face with a fresh surge of honeysuckle. It relaxed me under his invisible glare. "I came to see if your old friend's forgiveness was lost on you."

"As usual, I have no idea what you're talking about."

"Are your powers back, Gisel?"

"What powers?"

"The ones you used to turn on the water in your kitchen sink. The ones you've been searching for the last twenty years. The gift that only Helene could bestow upon you."

"Maybe Helene had nothing to do with it. If my daughter is a witch, her mother would have to be, too. Maybe the new coven has undone all of this."

His bitter laugh cut through me. "Oh, Gisel. You really think this can be undone by the ability to flip a light switch? Their husbands have all died." The energy drained from my being. I could almost feel it drip out of my toes as he took every ounce of hope from me. It was replaced by a need to hold on to my sisters. "Now you're getting it. You don't deserve her as a friend."

"Shut up!" I screamed at him. I held my head in my hands, squeezing the sides of my skull with my fingertips. "Get out of my house."

"I just wanted you to know that I'm watching."

"Why do you care?"

"Because unlike you, I care about her."

"I don't believe you."

He grabbed my arm and squeezed it in his cold hand. "Believe this. She may have forgiven you, but the curse is still in place. None of you will survive their daughters' husbands dying, too."

He couldn't know any of what he was saying. Lovie, Sloane, and Helene would never have breathed a word of this.

"They didn't have to say a word." I gritted my teeth at his comment. "If you don't figure a way out of this, having lost your powers for twenty years will feel like a vacation compared to what's coming."

"Impossible."

He let go of me. His footsteps moved away. "Wait until your son becomes the husband."

I launched my coffee mug in the direction of the despicable voice. It hit the wall, shattering and spewing coffee all over the pale blue paint. The back door opened. The air rushed out, taking the faint scent of honeysuckle with it.

I cleaned the wall. I was becoming an expert at erasing things. It had worked on the past while I'd been busy during the days. The life I'd lost fell into the background if I stayed in motion. It was the nights that killed me. I busied myself with Christmas decorations, baking, and addressing cards the entire day, but every time I walked by the damp paint in the kitchen, I knew my life was still in shambles.

Isaiah walked into our bedroom, red-faced and sweaty from working out.

"What are you doing? We're going to be late." I'd thought he was in the shower not in the basement lifting weights.

"I'm not going." He walked past me, into the bathroom, and turned on the water. He returned to our room without another word and searched through his drawers for some article of clothing that didn't matter since he was apparently staying home tonight.

"It's the Christmas concert." He didn't even look my way. "You would miss your daughter's show because of *her*? She's not going to hurt you. It's been twenty years." The delicate balance of our relationship had been upset by the return of Helene and her daughter. "Or is her hatred not what you're worried about?"

Isaiah finally faced me. "I'm not going to the concert," he said and closed the bathroom door behind him.

The minute Sloane and Lovie walked into the auditorium, the blood in my veins churned inside me. My coven was back, and tonight we'd be together. Waves of their energy floated across the seats between us and overcame me. Helene was nearby. I could feel her, too.

I forced air into my chest as my body heaved against its power. Helene took her seat on the side aisle. If I even looked at them, I'd launch to the ceiling, so I held my head in my hands and tried to calm down.

The beginning stanza of "O' Holy Night" filled the room, but what I felt was far from peace. I could burn the place down with the tip of my pointer finger. I couldn't decide what I missed more—my powers or my sisters. Either way, I was sure they were both there. Their daughters caught my eye on the stage as the storm raged outside the windows. It was the first time ever our two full covens were in the same place.

The deep growls of thunder almost drowned the voices singing. I was consumed by the fire in my fingers and the flight in my legs. I needed to escape the Christmas concert before something happened that I couldn't control. I stood and grasped the seat in front of me, clutching it. I turned and stared directly at Helene. Her eyes were dulled by a sadness I hadn't been with her to experience.

She stared back and almost knocked me over with a buried emotion: love. I wanted to shout it at her and Sloane and Lovie, to run to them and throw myself in their laps like a puppy, but my feet were solidly planted in place. The lights dimmed as the wind had its way outside, and a window cracked near the front of the auditorium. My head swirled around, and the storm broke into the room with us. The risers fell to the ground with the top row of singers following. The piano halted while parents and the choir director all ran to the stage.

None of it mattered. I covered my mouth with my hand, turned, and ran for the door. I was back in the same hallways I'd walked through as a teenager, and I was *back* to myself. The urge to scream from the top of the building that my powers had returned was eclipsed by the need to set something on fire. I ached to use all my powers at the same time. Command the elements and bring this town to its knees before me.

I ran out the side door and into the pouring rain. A bolt of lightning reached from the clouds to the stop sign on East Avenue. It highlighted my power, and as I raised my hand above my head, the tree across the street uprooted and fell on its side. *Ahhh.* I breathed in the storm around me and raging inside. I was intoxicated. While standing still, I swirled my arms high above my head, and the rain stopped falling upon me.

"Gisel." Helene's voice tried to steal me from my celebration. "Gisel, stop!"

"Don't you dare tell me to stop!" I screamed back at her. "Twenty years I've been without my powers. Twenty years!" I focused on the truck. It was large, but like the tree, it yielded to my whim. I flipped it on its side with a twirl of my wrist.

"Gisel, you have to calm down."

"What do you care?" I asked as I spun around to face my past.

"I never stopped caring about you. None of us have."

I'd longed to hear those words for so long that I'd convinced myself they'd never be true. The possibility cut me as I swallowed the notion down. "That isn't true." I shook my head.

"Your powers would only come back with our love." Helene was on the verge of tears. She was hurting, too. "I forgive you."

There was so much I wanted to say. I'd called out to them without a response for twenty years. I needed them as much as I loved them, but I couldn't face any of it tonight. My powers were overwhelming. I dropped my head back and stared at the raging sky. I belonged up there in it. I raised my arms above my head and clasped my hands before disappearing and flying over the school.

"Gisel." Helene's voice rang through the sky next to me.

I flew straight up and then balanced on the wind, lying flat on my stomach with my hands outstretched. Lovie and Sloane came and took Helene back inside, and I soared through the air. I flipped and turned, breathed in the frigid, wet air, and basked in the glorious sky. I flew to my mother's on Marlton Road and landed outside her back door.

She was sitting at the kitchen table playing solitaire the same way she did every other night of her lonely life. I opened the door and entered the kitchen, bringing with me the wind and rain that it carried.

"What the—" She placed her cards on the table and stared in my direction.

I showed myself. "It's me, Mama."

"Gisel." She stood, stepped away from the table, and walked over to touch my arms and shoulders. Her scrutiny focused in her small eyes that never let me out of her sight. "How?"

"Helene has forgiven me." Her hands released me and fell to her sides. "And with her forgiveness came my powers. I'm whole again."

"Well, I'll be damned." Her eyes filled with wonder at a love she'd stopped believing in decades ago.

"There's a tremendous chance of exactly that."

She rolled her eyes and found the old bottle of whiskey hidden among the cleaners stored under her sink. "This deserves a toast." She poured the brown syrup into two small juice glasses and handed me one.

"Mother, reverse the curse."

She threw her head back and downed her shot. "Can't be done." She dismissed me by returning to her seat and her deck of cards. Her knobby hands shuffled the cards over and over again.

"Of course it can be. You're a full coven. You can do anything."

She dropped the deck in disgust. "You have never considered the consequences. Where did I go wrong with you? You continue to live your life under the absurd assumption that no matter what you do, there will never be any ramifications."

"Mama. I'm not the one who did this. You are. You cast the spell—not me, not Helene or Sloane or Lovie. You are the one who didn't consider the ramifications. Undo it. Please."

"I'm serious. A witch's spell cannot be overturned. Period. These are the ways of the world, Gisel. Maybe if you'd taken a moment to think back then, there wouldn't have been a spell."

She was mad, but she couldn't put this on me. I'd face my own guilt tonight, in my bed, in the darkness. The same way I did every night, but I wouldn't take it from her. "If Helene can forgive me, you can forgive her."

"It's too late. Now, go on home and keep an eye on your husband and that son of yours. I'm sure your daughter is going to need you, too. If your powers are back, she must be thinking that she's gone insane."

I wanted her to stop talking about anything but how she was going to fix this. There had to be a way. My powers were back. My *coven* had returned. They were all waiting for me in Auburn. The rest of this could be undone. She stared down at the table, dismissing me.

"Some of us were born crazy," I mumbled under my breath as I slipped through the back door. I couldn't get away from her fast enough.

Mom. Her voice was in my head the moment my feet landed on our side yard.

Gwen, I thought and turned toward the house. Gwen appeared fifteen feet away from me. She was wearing her parka and the boots she'd had on at the concert. She looked toward the black sky and twirled her hand above her head. The rain flew away from her, leaving her dry beneath it. *Why didn't you tell me?*

How could I explain this before you'd experienced it?

I don't know, but I should have heard from you. Her voice was full of hurt and tinged with anger.

You're right. I'm sorry. I walked over to her and stepped into her dry spot with her. I pulled her close to me. My beautiful witch. "Let's go inside. It's been a long night already."

I put the teakettle on the back burner of the stove and slipped into my bedroom to change my clothes. Isaiah was asleep in our bed with the television on. The blue glow bounced on the wall above his head. I left it on and slipped into my robe.

Gwen poured us each a cup of hot chocolate. She sat at the kitchen table waiting for me to say something, but I had many questions, too.

"How did you find out?" I began with.

"Crazy things started happening. Fun stuff. Nothing too terrifying." She smiled, and it was the first time I realized she was a young woman. "But then I heard Ever in my head, and things started to scare me."

"What did she say?"

"She was calling for help." Gwen pressed her lips together the same way she used to when I tried to pry secrets out of her as a little girl.

I would let it go for now. "Do you like her?"

She nodded and took a sip of her hot chocolate. "Like I've known her my entire life. As if there isn't a secret she doesn't know and a moment we haven't shared. I feel that way about Maya and Ruby, too."

I closed my eyes and sank into my daughter's description of her coven. My interior had been hollowed out. I was empty inside without them.

"Which is crazy, because I've barely known them three months."

"You knew them before you were even born. The four of you were chosen to be together by the universe a million years ago. Not even the distance halfway around the earth could keep you apart."

"Why now? How come they've had their powers forever, and I'm just getting them now?"

I sat up straight as if the crown had been placed firmly on my head. "We are Earth witches. Had you been born a fire witch like Ruby, you'd have had your powers from the beginning." I didn't want to tell her everything. Not tonight. Maybe not ever. "But we gain our powers from the connection of the coven. We make each member stronger. Without us in the coven, they are less powerful. Without them, we are powerless."

"Why?"

"Why does a tree need water to live? Why do the bees pollenate the plants? It's the connectedness of the world and how we belong to it. It's the coven. The four of you were born to be together, whether you knew it or not."

"It's wonderful. I love having a coven."

"So did I."

Gwen tilted her head a little and examined me. She was far from the naive, flighty teenager she'd been in July. "You no longer have them?"

"I do. They were just gone for a very long time. Where did they move from?"

"Maya came from Hawaii. Ruby from Las Vegas, and Ever lived in Vermont. I guess they weren't really together, either."

"They were. It doesn't matter how far away you move as long as you still love each other. I know it's hard to believe. I didn't for a while, but distance doesn't matter. It's what's in your heart."

"Their hearts are broken. All three of their fathers died." Guilt choked me and drew the air back into my lungs. "Isn't that horrible?"

"Tragic." I considered telling Gwen the truth, but my fear for the way she'd look at me kept the words form leaving my mouth. I couldn't lose her, too.

"I thought that was why they seemed different at first. Something dark about them that could only come from the death of a parent, but I misread it. There's no darkness at all. Just a quiet sadness that surrounds them." Gwen tilted her cup until the last few drops made it into her mouth. She'd been completely excluded from the devastation she described.

"It's late."

"I have a million questions, though."

"I can't wait to answer all of them, but not tonight." I pointed at the clock on the microwave that read twelve forty-nine.

VII

You can't change the future by ignoring the past.
Buried secrets will always rise again.

CHRISTMAS WAS MAGICAL. IKE AND Gwen's first Christmases, and the ones that followed when they'd still been in awe of the bows and ornaments and twinkling lights almost compared to this year's. It was hard to measure up to the universe's gifts being returned to me.

I woke early every morning and practiced my craft. Moving things, commanding the elements, disappearing at will, it all came back to me as if it'd never left. I inhaled my power with every breath and I, too, forgave. Without all the bitterness and loneliness to anchor me to the ground, I could imagine myself as a different woman. One who dealt in possibilities and the future, rather than the losses of the past.

My morning rituals since the school concert included my calling to Helene after I brushed my teeth. I took a moment of silence in my master bath and thought her name the same way I had thousands of times after she'd left. I considered calling to Sloane or Lovie, or just driving over to Auburn and knocking on their door, but there was still so much unresolved, and it all began with Helene and me.

Helene. I spread my lips wide around my clean and flossed teeth. *Helene.* I rubbed in tiny dabs of primer to my face and walked out of the bathroom while it dried. *Helene.*

I thought her name a few more times as I pulled a pair of jeans out of the drawer. I was practically singing it and more focused on whether to wear the cowl neck sweater or if it'd be too hot as I rambled off, *Helene, I want to see you. I need to talk to you.*

Yes, she thought back.

The gray sweater I'd just pulled off my shelf fell to the floor. My body almost followed it down.

I leaped into the air and danced into my bedroom with my eyes closed. I froze, not sure if she was saying yes to seeing me, or just responding.

Yes, you'll see me?

Yes. Not here, though. Not in Auburn . . . and not there.

Well, yeah. No kidding. Isaiah couldn't even handle the Christmas concert. He'd bang a hole in the ice and throw himself into the frozen lake if Helene rang our doorbell.

Meet me at the winery tonight at six o'clock.

Okay. Isaiah, the kids, and I had gone to the winery for my last birthday. I'd hated every birthday since my coven had left, but I'd smiled and ate my pizza. I'd drunk the wine, but nothing Isaiah could ever come up with was going to be a reason to celebrate my life without my sisters.

I arrived early and picked out a table near the fireplace. I thought Helene would like it. Part of me thought the table farthest from the door would be better. Anyone who saw us was going to stop by and chat about high school and today. Both of which were pretty much the same subject since nothing ever changed in this town. There was a brutal chill in the wind, so the fireplace won out.

"Hi. Welcome to Auburn Road," the waitress said, as if this meeting weren't my own personal equivalent of a global summit, a healing surgery, and spiritual awakening all at the same time. "Here's a menu."

I took it from her, mainly for Helene because I didn't need it. I wasn't eating. Only drinking. "We'll take a bottle of Good Karma."

"Two glasses?"

"Yes." She could have just brought me the bottle . . . and poured it into my mouth. I needed karma and everything else on my side. Even with my powers back, there was still so much riding on this. I wanted my coven back, too. I missed them so desperately it hurt to be awake some days. Their return had freshened the pain of their departure. I'd buried those feelings with the loss of my powers.

The waitress delivered the bottle with two glasses. She removed the menus sitting on the table in front of me. Our hands collided as I reached for the bottle. There was an urgent need for the deep red elixir to enter my body.

"Sorry," I said without looking up. I was too busy filling my glass.

The door opened, and Helene took a step into the room. The energy coursing between us at the Christmas concert and the storm raging outside had masked her beauty. She'd always been sophisticated. Even when she wore gym shorts and a sweatshirt, Helene was exotic and refined. I would have paled in comparison, but she spread her light wide and shined on everyone around her.

I ripped myself from my stunned admiration and poured her a glass of wine. The least I could do was let her have a few sips before I downed the whole bottle.

"I can't stay long," she said.

It was a fresh insult. She wouldn't be able to share her presence at length. "Leaving is your specialty," I lightly said. I didn't come to argue.

"How's your mother?" Apparently, Helene had.

My attention dropped toward the table. Any hope of mending the rift and being invited back to Auburn flew out the door she'd just walked through.

I inhaled deeply and found the strength to face my lost friend. "I'm sorry." She sat across from me without a word or an expression or a chance. "I hated you for leaving me." That was just the beginning, though. "I'm grateful you came home. I love you. I need you." Tears filled my eyes. For so long I've wanted to say those words to her. "I—"

"I forgive you," she said. In all our years as best friends, she'd never forgiven because there'd never been anything to be sorry for. What I'd done should have been unforgivable, but there she was, offering it to me.

I wiped away my tears and rested my face in my hands. The exhaustion the last twenty years had caused fell on my shoulders by the fire in the winery. "Thank you." She'd given me a future, even though I felt as if I'd stolen her own. "Not just for me, but for my daughter."

Helene's breath caught. She didn't know Gwen. "What's her name?"

"Gwen." I couldn't wait for them to meet her. We should get all of the girls together. It was their birthright, and we were all blessed to have them.

"Have the girls met her?" She had no idea they were friends.

"Of course. They were at her birthday party."

"Of course." Helene nodded but was lost in thought. "Do you think they know?" She didn't have to say, "about their coven" or, "how they belong to each other."

The real question was how could Helene not know, but nothing had changed for her in the way of her daughter's powers. She hadn't been watching every breath Ever had taken for the last seventeen years, hoping to capture a glimpse of the abilities. "I knew when Gwen was born that she was a witch, but her powers didn't fully emerge until she found her coven."

"I'm sorry, Gisel."

One thing my mother was right about was that we'd all known the pain caused that fateful day. The thought of my mother brought back the horrid reasons this reconciliation was so difficult. "What now?"

"Ever is grounded. She isn't allowed to see your son." Thank God. I took a sip of my wine. More guilt. It would have pulled me under, but my powers returning kept me afloat. Helene was protecting my son by not allowing him to see her daughter. There was no way for me to return the gesture. No one could protect their daughters from the history that was destined to be their future. "And the Virago doesn't condone forgiveness."

The wine soured in my throat at the mention of their name. "They've been running wild since you guys left."

"I'd assumed you'd be one of them by now."

I stared at Helene in outrage. "I would never." I shook my head. "They tried, but I'd rather live alone."

"You weren't alone, though." Her words cut through me.

I had Isaiah. "I'm so sorry, Helene." I twirled my wine glass by the stem between my fingers. "I'm ashamed." I couldn't look at her. My gaze fell to the table, and I shut my eyes tight to avoid seeing the hurt in her eyes. "That night—"

"I can't." Her voice was low and filled with resolve. "I need to just move forward. Okay?"

"You know that'll never work. If you didn't know it before, you realized the day you chose to come home."

"I'm going to go. I'm glad your powers are back."

"I'm alive again. It's as if the only things real from the last twenty years are my children. The rest was half a life without you and Sloane and Lovie." She had to believe me. It was the only truth left. That and the fact that the spell could not be undone. Their daughters would hate me and my mother. Their hatred would carry to Gwen, too. Or, even worse, Gwen would hate me for what I'd done and she would leave to be with her coven. We could never be a family again because of the events I set in motion. "I love you, Helene."

She smiled. It appeared painful, contorting her face into that almost pleasant expression toward me. She didn't invite me back to Auburn or pull me into her arms, but she forgave me. It was a new day.

I bought two bottles of wine to go and raced home to Alloway. When I got there, Tommy's new truck was in the driveway. He hadn't been over since he'd bought it. That was the kind of friends Tommy and Isaiah were. When either of them got a new car, they brought it by to show the other one. It was just one of the many things Angie and I made fun of them for.

I didn't feel like dealing with Tommy, but I was sure they heard my car pull in, so I closed the garage door behind me and went inside. No one was in the house. Their laughter came through the back doors, which were wide open allowing the smell of smoke from the fire to float in with the wind. I stepped out back.

"There she is," Tommy said.

"Where have you been?" Angie asked, and Isaiah gave me a look as to say, "Yeah, where *have* you been?"

In that instant, my invitation for our old friends to come over for drinks came back to me. "I'm so sorry. Everything's been crazy around here with the holidays. I completely forgot. Let me open some wine and fix some snacks."

"You don't have to do that," Angie said. "Well, the snacks anyway.

You're going to need some wine."

"Why's that?" I relaxed a little.

"Because we were just telling Isaiah that Helene and Lovie and Sloane are back in town." Of course. The whole town must already know. I nodded involuntarily. "Mick is in a few classes with Helene's girl, and I think he has a crush on Lovie's." Angie laughed the same way she did in ninth grade. "Isn't that funny? Mick is such a sweetie. I can totally see him with Lovie's daughter."

My chest tightened. I couldn't breathe. None of this was funny. "I can see that, too." Angie and the rest of the town had no idea how dangerous it was to love these girls. Except for my mother. She knew, and she didn't care.

"Have you seen them?" Angie wasn't really close to any of us, but she knew the whole story. Well, not the whole story. She'd been Tommy's girlfriend when it'd all gone down. She knew Isaiah had cheated on Helene with me and that Helene had left us both. That was about twenty percent of the truth, and it still seemed like enough to write a tragic novel about.

"I have." I searched my mind for what a normal person would say. "They look great."

"They always did." Angie cuddled in closer to Tommy on the loveseat. A piece of wood fell farther into the fire, and sparks flew up in the air. Angie's hand slipped down the inside of Tommy's thigh, and he kissed the top of her head. Even after all these years and three boys, he still kissed her like they were in high school.

"I need some wine."

"I'll help you," Isaiah said. I had the distinct feeling I was in trouble. I just didn't know why. "I'm thirsty," he said and looked back at his best friend and his wife as he walked through the back door. "Where were you?" he asked as soon as we cleared the doorway.

"What does it matter?" I attempted to seem appalled. I might have even rolled my eyes. "Since when do you have to know where

I am every second?"

Isaiah grabbed me by my upper arms and stared at me before slowly asking again, "Where were you?"

"Get off me." I inhaled deeply, smelling for liquor to explain his anger, but the only thing I could smell was smoke.

"Tell me, Gisel."

I threw him across the room. He hit the wall with his shoulder but stayed on his feet. Isaiah was still in great shape. "Did I mention my powers are back?"

"She forgave you?"

"They all did."

"And that's where you were tonight? With *them*?"

I tried to make sense of the emotions in my head. I wasn't jealous. I knew he still loved her, and I'd had a lifetime to accept that. I wasn't hiding it from him because I was afraid of him. It was something else. Some instinctual protection of our marriage, because it had to be real. "I was with Helene."

Isaiah stared at me with fire in his eyes, but it wasn't directed at me. It was her name. I'd ignited a hundred-year-old blaze inside him. One there was nothing I could do to put out.

"Did she say anything about me?" My husband was a broken man. His voice was low and rough leaving his lips.

"Need help?" Tommy asked as he walked between us. He opened the fridge and grabbed two beers out of it. "Do you guys have something I can ash in?" He pulled a pack of cigarettes out of his coat pocket.

"There's a bucket next to the swing out there."

He nodded and left us in the kitchen without an ounce of understanding of the ways in which our marriage was disintegrating.

"She didn't," I said. I felt guilty about that, too.

History's a hellion.

THE MONTHS FLEW BY. HELENE and I had every adult we knew that worked in the high school keeping an eye on our kids. They could be friends, but they couldn't date and they absolutely weren't allowed to fall in love. Gwen and I focused on her learning the craft. She was . . . unpredictable. There wasn't anything she wasn't willing to try. She did hesitate when I first asked her to fly with me. I had to pry out of her the strange experience she'd had when Ever had first taken her. I made a note to schedule a meeting with Helene, Lovie, and Sloane about the Virago. It sounded as if they had a lot to share.

I shouldn't have had to make an appointment to see them. We should have been together. I'd been forgiven, but not brought back into our group. The three of them were over there, and I was in Alloway with my husband. I didn't know how to get them back. Card games, wine and dine, greeting cards. None of it was going to erase the fact that their husbands were dead and mine—who also happened to be the first boy Helene ever loved—was still alive. The creepy invisible guy was right—I needed to find a way to reverse the curse or none of us would ever truly have our lives back.

Ever's birthday came and went without an invitation. I watched Ike like a prison warden on the day. If they were still seeing each other, he'd be with her on her birthday, but he didn't even try to leave the house. Dave Anzaldo asked Gwen to the prom, but Ike never mentioned going. Not even after I interrogated him about girls, dances, graduation, and specifically Ever.

His answers always ranged from "I don't want to talk about it" to "This is stupid." Isaiah finally convinced me to drop it. A subject he'd ignored for weeks was suddenly one he felt knowledgeable enough to weigh in on. I'd spent the night with my mother at her house. We'd come to the painful conclusion that she could no longer stay there alone. I was telling Isaiah about her application at the Friends Home when Ike blew by us without saying hello.

"What's his deal?"

"He's fine." Isaiah had answered too quickly.

I studied my husband. He had bags under his eyes as if he hadn't slept, but there was something youthful about him. He was excited. "Like how . . . fine?"

"Like, give the kid a break. He's doing great in school and has been accepted to college and maybe we should give him some space, fine."

"I told you he's not to see Ever Ayars."

"I heard you when you said it." Isaiah got up and left the room without another word.

Something was going on. For the next few weeks, I increased my surveillance duty, and I combined my efforts with the rest of my coven in Auburn. Helene swore Ever was properly locked down. According to her, they were miserable because of it, and it sounded like she was talking about the entire house.

I was making a list of all the plants I wanted to get at La Rosa's. This spring, I was going to light the yard up in a way it hadn't been since Isaiah and I had moved in. Hydrangeas, roses, daylilies, blue sage, and daffodils. Gwen would be ecstatic when she saw them all in bloom. My cell phone rang just as I lowered my pen in satisfaction at my plan. "Hello."

"Hi, Gisel. This is Trish. I was just calling to confirm Ike's absence. Is he not feeling well?" My chest tightened. "There are quite a few students out today. Must be something going around." Ike's morning ran through my mind. Nothing was amiss. He'd been on his way to school the last time I saw him. The thought of him on the side of the road wouldn't stick in my mind. He was with Ever Ayars. "It's these warm winters. *Everyone* is sick."

"Yes," I said. I didn't want the school to know anything about Ike's whereabouts until I found him myself. "Thanks for calling, Trish."

"Tell him we hope he feels better. I have to go call the rest of these parents who forgot to let the school know."

"Sorry, Trish."

"No worries. Gives me a chance to catch up with people."

I pressed end on the call. *Helene*. It was after nine, so I figured she would be awake. When she didn't answer right away, I tried again. *Helene!*

I was going to sit at my kitchen table and continue to yell inside my head until Helene answered. The back door opened, and I exhaled the anxiety Trish's phone call had caused. Isaiah walked in and stared at me. "Have you heard from Ike?"

He shook his head never taking his eyes off me. "No. He's not at school?"

"No. Trish called."

"Well, I just picked up the fertilizer in town, and he wasn't anywhere to be found. So you don't have to worry he's been in an accident."

"I wasn't. I'd know if he were hurt." Isaiah nodded. He was getting used to my returned powers and my delight in them. "He's with her."

He paused for an infantile second. "Who?"

Lord, he annoyed me. "Ever. Helene's daughter. Don't act like you don't know who I mean or what's going on."

Gisel, Trish just called. Is Ike out, too?

I turned away from my husband to focus on Helene.

Yes.

We're going to go looking for them. Stay there, and if Ike comes home, let me know.

Okay. I wanted to be with them. *Helene?*

Yes.

Keep in touch.

We will.

I turned my frustration back on Isaiah. "As soon as he gets home, I'm taking that motorcycle away from him forever."

"It won't help."

"Why not?" He was never going to be with Ever Ayars. I wouldn't risk him for anything. Not even Helene's daughter.

"Because nothing you say or do is going to keep them apart." Isaiah was infuriating.

"You don't know that."

"No, *you* don't know that, because you've never been in love the way they are." I stopped existing for a second and let his words in. "In your youth, when the whole world balanced on the sound of your lover's breath while they touched your skin." I held on to the table in front of me to balance myself while my husband described an obsession I'd never been privy to. "When you'd risk losing everything to spend a moment alone with that person."

Yesterday, I'd thought I couldn't hate him more, but it was possible. "It's not like that. They barely know each other." Isaiah raised his eyebrows and dipped his head toward me in argument. "She's just the 'new girl' from out of town. Ike's curious about her."

"You'll never understand." Isaiah seemed to know a great deal more than I did about our son and Helene's daughter.

Instead of hurling the table at him and screaming at him to shut up, I walked out of the room without another word to my *beloved* husband.

Helene checked in with me every thirty minutes or so, but the seconds that ticked by between her updates were dreadful. So, to distract myself, I pulled the attic steps down from the corner of Gwen's room and ascended the stairs to my past. Behind the high chair and wedding boxes were the two trunks I hadn't been able to open since I'd filled them when I was eighteen. They held the memories of my life as a young girl—a young witch.

From the attic window, I could see Isaiah spreading the fertilizer over the lawn. Fresh buds littered the branches of the tress. The grounds around us were set to explode. I removed the lid on the box labeled "Childhood" and rummaged through school photos, 4-H ribbons, ceramic molds of my hands, and old report cards. Near the bottom was a pile of pictures of the four of us. Our mothers had taken us to the beach, the zoo, the park, anywhere we could listen to the wind and watch the sky. Halfway through the pile, I found my favorite. A photo of the four of us in front of a fire in the backyard of my house. Our arms were around each other. The flames rose up behind us, and we were smiling with our eyes closed. The heat rose up my neck as the tears filled my eyes. We were proper witches back then. Nothing could separate us. I exhaled.

"Gisel," Isaiah called up from Gwen's room.

Even the sound of his voice annoyed me. "What?"

"I'm going out to look for him. Make sure he's not in a ditch somewhere."

"Whatever."

As Isaiah climbed into his truck, I watched from the attic window and thought what it would be like if *he* ended up in a ditch somewhere. I shook the idea away. *Consequences, Gisel. He's your children's father.* I needed to be more careful this time around.

I left the attic and made triple chocolate chip cookies from scratch for Isaiah. They were my apology for a mental discretion he didn't know about. They were Ike's favorite, too, but these I felt I owed my husband. A wish he would die exchanged for three flavors of chocolate mixed together with batter. Things were always so simple in my head compared to everyone else's.

Gisel.

Yes. I dropped the spatula into the bowl and wiped the remnants of the batter from the corner of my mouth. *Have you found them?*

No. Why don't you come over? Wait for them here.

In Auburn. A warmth rose in my chest and welled into tears in my eyes. The offer was more than significant. I hadn't been to Auburn in years. Living in Alloway, there was no reason to drive through the little town unless I wanted to torture myself, which only happened about once a year.

I didn't know how to phrase my next question. Or if it should even be asked—ever.

What about Isaiah? I finally managed to think.

Helene was silent until I thought she'd moved on from our conversation, but then she thought back, *Bring him. He's your husband and Gwen and Ike's father. He belongs here with us.*

My eyes darted around the room, searching for evidence that what I'd just heard had been said. There had to have been a witness. My eyes shut. I was alone in the house, but I wasn't alone in life any longer. They'd invited me back. My chest tightened, and sobs racked my body as I tried to comprehend the enormity of Helene's forgiveness. She was so much better than I was.

The scene my husband walked in on must have looked utterly insane. When he'd left me, I could barely stand the sight of him. Since he'd been gone, I'd chosen to bake. The aroma of chocolates surrounded the absurdity. The cookies cooled on the racks by the sink. I was dressed and waiting for him at the kitchen table. Confusion was a common expression for Isaiah, especially when it came to me. He'd spent his entire adult life trying to navigate the journey with a woman he never really understood.

"What's . . . going on?"

"No sign of them?"

A moment fell between his words and belied information he wasn't sharing. "No." I didn't believe him, but Isaiah wasn't capable of keeping Ike's whereabouts from me. "What are you doing?"

"I made you cookies." His brow furrowed as he glanced at the cookies and back at me. "We're going to Auburn." He froze in front of me, and then his shoulders sank as he exhaled. "They'll come back soon. It's just a skipped day of school."

"I know. They're not who I'm worried about."

He was unsalvageable. Drove me nuts since . . . "You should be. Your son impregnating that girl should be your only concern."

"Why? This insanity has nothing to do with them."

"Of course it does. The curse will be handed down for every generation to come."

"What?" Isaiah yelled and then let his mouth hang open in disgust. "Gwen and the girls are fine. She's never been happier. Why would it have anything to do with them?"

"Because when my mother cast that curse it wasn't meant to stop with Helene, Sloane, and Lovie. It was meant to affect every heir in their bloodlines. Do that math. If our son falls in love with Ever and they have a child, he's going to die."

"I'm so *sick* of your coven and its *craft*." He spewed the words in my direction. "I'll be in the truck."

We rode in silence through the town of Woodstown and the fields on the other side. Isaiah's grip on the steering wheel tightened when we passed the entrance to Laurel Hills. His mother still lived back there, just up the crick from Auburn. My eyes narrowed on him, and my hand tightened around the plate of warm cookies I held in my lap. A peace offering for my husband that I was taking back and giving to my sisters.

"You know where they are." I launched my accusation at him as he drove.

Isaiah didn't move, and he never looked away from the road. "Don't be ridiculous."

"You know!" I wasn't being ridiculous. "What else do you know?"

"Gisel." He shook his head, dismissing me.

"Where are they?" My blood boiled beneath the surface of my skin.

"I don't know where, but they're together. You're underestimating how he feels about her."

"Stop. It's impossible." I wouldn't listen to another word of it. Helene and I had kept them apart. There were hundreds of girls in Woodstown High School. Ike was not going to end up with Ever or anyone else cursed in this town.

He turned toward Auburn and seemed to age five years before my eyes. I couldn't think about him or what this was costing him. I had to focus on Ike and finding him.

He didn't ask which house was theirs or bother to hide that he already knew exactly which house she was in. He just turned into Sloane's parents' home at the end of the road.

Lovie came running out the back door as soon as my feet were beneath me on the ground.

"Gisel," she said and pulled me against her chest. Isaiah took the plate of cookies from my hand, and I hugged her back. "I'm glad you're here." I'd missed her, her hair, the warm brown color of her eyes, the decency that surrounded her, and most of all the affection.

"Welcome home," Sloane said from behind her.

I knew better than to hug her. Sloane wasn't the type. "I could say the same to you," I said instead.

Lovie silently hugged Isaiah. Sloane practically ignored him, which made him smile slightly. He'd always loved the way Sloane didn't take anything from anyone. She made a sport of grudge holding.

We all followed Sloane inside to where Helene was waiting in the kitchen. Sloane, Lovie, and I stood paralyzed as Helene and Isaiah stared at each other, and our pasts threatened to swallow the five of us whole.

When the weight of their heartache threatened to infect me, I thought, *Helene, are you okay?*

She turned to me and blushed. The deep berry-colored scarf wrapped around her neck accentuated the noble green of her eyes.

Helene.

She barely nodded, but it was so slight I doubted Isaiah caught it. He was an outsider. The way he always should have been.

"No word?" I said aloud, and the five of us moved toward the table that had been in the kitchen since we were little.

"No," Sloane said and was the first to sit down.

"I'll get some tea," Lovie said and avoided being trapped in a seat with the heavy past that surrounded us. The tea couldn't save her, though. She was every bit a part of this as we were.

Helene's gaze flew around the room, inspecting everything but my husband. She lowered her head into her hands and held perfectly still. She was talking to Ever. I leaned forward on the table as if I could climb inside her and hear, too. Helene's hands slipped farther back on her head until she finally looked up and said, "They're coming."

The back door opened and Gwen, Maya, and Ruby joined us in the kitchen. Gwen was completely at ease as if she'd been in the kitchen a hundred times before.

"Where did you come from?" I asked her.

Gwen's gaze traveled around the room taking in every occupant including her father. "Have you met Maya and Ruby?" she asked. When I shook my head, she added, "My water and fire witches."

Their eyes darted between each other. Tiny nods of their heads gave away the conversation they were having without us. "Nice to meet you. I saw you at Gwen's birthday party."

"How come you're here?" I asked again.

"Ever called us. She said she was on her way home."

"Let me guess," Sloane said. "You three have been avoiding Auburn until you heard from her."

Our daughters didn't say a word. They were their own coven. They belonged to Ever as much as they did to us. Ruby only smiled before grabbing a glass out of the cabinet and handing it to Gwen.

Ever walked into the crowded kitchen with Ike following. My eyes closed as I inhaled the full power of two covens. I could feel every groove in the table's wood beneath my fingers. It was the beautiful madness that had been missing since their grandmothers had died. Since my mother was the only member left of our ancestor's living coven. Ever swallowed hard and looked to Ruby.

"I know," Ruby said. "It's like we've been running on forty percent."

Sloane rubbed her daughter's shoulders and said, "If Clara were here, I'm not sure I could stand to be inside, but man it feels good to be this powerful again." She shook her head with satisfaction covering her face.

"You two were in love?" Ever scrutinized Isaiah as she asked. He didn't respond, but it wasn't necessary. One could tell from his tortured existence anywhere near Helene that he loved her still.

"Dad?" Ike asked, and I watched as Helene nearly crumbled. Their reunion shouldn't include our children.

"A long time ago," he finally said. Helene looked his way without a word. The tension and years of unspoken words rushed past me and between the two of them. I was tired of being the center of their failed love affair and I hated that I was the cause of it.

"None of this matters," I said. The only thing that needed to be addressed today was my son staying away from Helene's daughter. I pointed at the two of them. "You two are done."

Ike stepped out from behind Ever and positioned himself in front of her. His movements were natural. Their bodies were accustomed to being near one another, and the way he blocked her from the rest of us forced my heart down to the depths of my being.

"Oh my God." I practically fell into my seat. "You love her." I turned to Helene. "How could you let this happen?"

"*Let?* I have forbidden her to be anywhere near him."

Isaiah's claims that I'd never understand this type of love slapped me again. I was in over my head with my son and his first love. "What are we going to do?"

"We're going to tell them, and then we're going to get rid of it," Sloane said and sat across from me at the table.

What good would telling them do? Another generation haunted by their future. This couldn't be escaped, and Sloane knew it. "We can't change the spell. It was cast by a full coven. To change it, even if we could, *which* we *can't*, would interrupt the entire universe. We'll set into motion horrors we can't even predict."

A fierce cold darted off Sloane as she fixed her eyes on me. "That's easy for you to say as your husband sits at the table with us." It was the latest gash in my abdomen of wounds. I'd nearly killed myself with hate over the years.

Anger poured out of the holes they'd left in me. "I begged her not to!" I yelled. "I have searched the world for a way to reverse it. Read every piece of information and talked to every witch that would speak to me."

Lovie came and rested her hands on the table as she stood above all of us. "This isn't helping."

She was right. For the first time, we were all sitting around the same table. We'd come this far. "You can't just stop a spell. You'll unhinge this whole town."

"What spell?" Ever asked.

She was fearless. I wondered if she'd still be after today. I turned to face her mother, who said, "You should tell them." It was generous, considering. My children needed to know the truth, too, but some stories of their parents' youth shouldn't be handed down.

I left the security of my coven's stare and turned to face Ruby, Maya, and Ever. They didn't deserve this. "Our coven's history has not been an easy one." I started with the easy lesson. "Your grandmothers and Gwen's grandmother were also a coven."

I wrung my hands before placing them flat on the table in front of me. I didn't want them to hate me. I was tired of the contempt. "Lovie's mother died when she gave birth to Lovie . . ." I paused to check on Lovie. She'd lived her entire life without her mother. The mention of her now was no offense. "Which left three members of the coven. Gwen's, Ruby's, and Ever's grandmothers." I looked around the familiar kitchen. The house had been a part of all of our families for generations. "And then, one day when we were in high school, Sloane and Helene's mothers—Ruby and Ever's grandmothers—went to the shore." Helene's head dropped, but I continued. "Their car was hit head on by a tractor trailer, and they both died."

No one made a sound. Half of us knew what was coming; the other half couldn't imagine it. I could barely breathe. "My mother was alone for the first time in her life," I continued. "She never got over it. She felt abandoned. The loneliness without her sisters ate her alive inside." I had some firsthand knowledge of her pain. "Our last year in high school was turbulent. Between the four of us, we had one mother, and she was angry. A lot happened." I forced myself to face Helene. "Some terrible things happened that I regret every day. When Sloane and Helene and Lovie were planning to go away for college and leave me here alone . . . without my powers, my mother became enraged. She took out all her anger on the three of them. She wanted them to feel the same pain she saw inflicted on me."

I searched Gwen's eyes for understanding. This was her blood we were talking about. I wanted to run, to hide in Alloway and never speak the words, but it wouldn't end. Our only hope was the truth. "And she cursed them."

"Mimi?" Gwen wailed.

"What was the curse?" Ruby demanded. She was ready to lunge at someone.

I waited for someone else to speak. There must have been a person in the room with the strength that I was missing, but no one said a word. Their silence forced out, "That death would hunt their children's fathers."

"I don't understand," Maya whispered.

"Yes, you do," Ruby said, and Maya began to shake as understanding settled inside her. Her hands clenched into fists at her side as her chest gasped for tiny breaths. She ran past us and up the stairs.

Ike turned around. He took Ever's face in his hands, and the tears welled in my eyes. He held her still as if he could will her to forgive us.

"Ever," Helene said and took control of the room. "Do you understand why you can't see him?"

"He didn't do this," Ever said, and the pain in her voice was too much to bear.

"It's as much about him as it is about us," Helene said, but Ever shook her head, still not grasping the endurance of our hell.

"The spell is meant to carry to our daughters, too. If you and Ike continue seeing each other, get married . . . if you ever have a child, Ike will die."

"And you'll wait for it to happen," Sloane said. I thought I might throw up. This was worse than I'd ever imagined. In all the years they'd been away, I'd hoped if we ever could get back together, we could make us whole again and reverse what my mother had done. It was too late, though. They'd lost too much and would never be able to see me as anything more than the cause of this. "You'll wait for the day your daughter will bury her father every day that he's still alive."

"That's why you never came back? Vermont, Hawaii, Vegas? You tried to outrun it," Ever said.

"Yes." Helene answered her daughter's question with strength and resolve. "We tried everything."

"And that's why it seemed like you were expecting it?" Ever's eyes overflowed with love for her mother. "How did you live that way?" she asked all three of them.

"With hope," Helene said. "Always with hope, but when Maya's father died, we knew we had to come back here. The three of you were starting to fall in love. You've already lost your fathers. We can't watch you bury your husbands."

"But there's no way to stop it," I said.

"If we need a full coven to cast a spell, how could Ike's grand-mother curse us?" Ever asked.

"She's a full coven. Her sisters died." Helene answered for all of us. Her jaw tightened as she further explained, "She hadn't been denounced or left behind. Clara being alone was a natural part of life. Her powers remained completely intact. Dangerously so."

"She couldn't just kill you." It wasn't a question. Ever already understood the limits imposed by our birthright.

"Even in her bitterness, Clara was still a witch. In her head, she was an honorable one. She would never impact another witch's mortality. Not even the ones she cursed to live a life in hell."

"Oh."

"She did the next worst thing. She tortured us by taking away someone we loved." Helene stared back at Isaiah. He was mine. They'd lost their husbands, and I still had him. It was cruel.

"Well, we're going to figure it out," Lovie said. Everyone's attention fell on her. "Together. We're a coven—two covens." She considered Ruby, Gwen, and Ever as if they were her own. "And we're not leaving here until the spell is broken." She was nodding, willing us to commit. When the room calmed, she said, "We need to eat. I'll bread some eggplant."

Fall onto us when you need to.
We'll always catch you.

THE DAYS RUSHED BY. WE were trying to cure a disease before it infected us all and killed us one by one. The guilt of having my powers back overshadowed everything I did with my coven. I'd always have my powers, and every daughter to be born into my family would have hers, but their husbands would keep dying. Sloane, Lovie, and Helene never spoke a word of what I was thinking. They avoided it on purpose because they were kind. If they'd wanted to inflict more pain on me, there would have been no point in forgiving me.

"How come you didn't tell me this nightmare would be passed down to every future generation?" Isaiah asked. He sat at the island and sipped his coffee. He never took his eyes off me. His calm demeanor bespoke of the grotesque past we shared. I'd rather he yelled. Thrown something at me perhaps. I deserved all of it, and if it weren't going to come from Auburn, I'd take it from him. "Gisel."

I sat on the stool beside him. "What does it matter? Nothing is going to happen to Gwen."

"It matters because they were my friends, too. I was a part of this, and I never really knew the extent of it."

"I didn't keep it from you on purpose. I just couldn't tell you."

"Why? Because you couldn't trust me?"

I closed my eyes. I couldn't face him. Any of them. They must have all thought I caused this, and they were right. "Because I couldn't stand to say the words aloud."

"There are lots of people to blame for this." He took the last sip of his coffee. "The shame of it is that not one of them is a junior in high school. Those girls have done nothing and they've been through enough."

I closed my eyes. "I can't imagine."

"I wonder if your mother could. If she had any idea of what she was inflicting on them."

A bitter lump lodged in my throat. I swallowed it down. "I think she knew." I stood straight and repositioned the wall inside me I'd erected to separate my mother's hideous curse from any evil I was capable of. I'd been reckless, but I'd never been heartless. "I just don't think she cared."

Isaiah left me in the kitchen. I watched from the window as he pulled a canoe off the lawn and into the lake. Every time he'd taken one out by himself, I'd thought he was thinking of her. I knew they'd gone canoeing even before they'd been a couple. Helene and Isaiah had always been a couple of something. She used to laugh so hard at his jokes, I'd thought that alone would keep them together forever. I barely laughed with him. He didn't amuse me the way he did her.

As for Mama, she continued to deteriorate. I wasn't even sure if I loved her anymore. There was a part of me that continued to dutifully care for her, but all the other parts had withered and blown away when I was left in Auburn by myself. She was even more unreasonable in her convalescence than she'd been when she was vibrant.

"There has to be something you can do," I whispered near her ear when the aide had finally left her room at the nursing home I'd moved her into. "Some way to change this."

She rolled her old, sunken, bloodshot eyes. "You're a fool. Just because they've taken you back doesn't mean a thing."

I sat back and stared at her sternly. "You're wrong. It means everything. What if one of them falls in love with a witch? What will happen then?"

"Don't be ridiculous. Witches can't be men. You know that."

"It's a new time, Mama. Women fall in love with women every day."

"Poppycock. Bunch of—"

"And I've met a man who's something very close to a witch."

She pulled herself up against her pillow. "Who?" She'd abandoned sexual orientation for a topic she was intrigued by.

"I don't know his name. He comes to the house sometimes." Her stare bore into me. "I can't ever see him, but he's read my mind."

Her sharp inhale clued me into the fact that Helene's name shouldn't be mentioned anywhere near this topic. If my mother was afraid of him and knew he claimed to be Helene's friend, she'd help even less with her awful spell. "What does he say?"

I sat back and put some space between us. "He speaks as if he's known us all for a long time. As if he's been watching us." I lowered my head. "He knows what I've done."

"How can you be sure it's a man if you've never seen him?"

"How could I be sure if I had seen him?" I asked, and her jaw tightened. Infuriating her had some appeal to me even in her last days. "I sensed he was a man. A large, powerful, slightly sinister man."

"Well, if there is such a thing, he'd have to be part of the Virago."

"Why?"

"Because that's where all the outcasts go. No coven would include a man."

The fate of a man born as a witch stayed with me the rest of the day until just before dinner. I turned to my phone sitting on the counter and could sense the darkness before it rang. It was the Friends Home calling to say Mama had passed away. She'd been alone.

How fitting.

Mama's loneliness was her only companion the second half of her life. Not even her grandchildren could save her from it. She was a different woman after her coven died. Watching her deteriorate helped keep me sane when I was alone. In a way, her bitter anger made me stronger. I'd never joined the Virago because I never let myself sink to the depths of my mother's despair.

"Do you need anything?" Lovie asked when she called.

"No." I shook my head, even though she couldn't see me. It was too much to ask them to be involved in anything that had to do with her.

"She was your mother." She was also the last of her coven. There should be some special burial ceremony when a coven was lost to the earth. "That's more important than anything else she ever did."

"Lovie, you're the most decent human being I've ever known."

This made her laugh, which lightened the putrid atmosphere surrounding me. "Just know we're here if you need anything." She left off how between the three of them they knew more about grief and mourning and burials than any woman ever should.

"Uncle Stump is coming tomorrow, and the services will be Friday."

"Send our love to him, and we'll be there."

It was the end of their mothers' coven, too. The end of it all, but I still couldn't shake the notion that Mama would somehow fly from her coffin and punish us for being together and happy. I wondered if she was in heaven, finally reunited with her sisters. If she was drinking whiskey and toasting the eight of us down here.

Isaiah's hands dug into my shoulders the way he used to massage them when I'd been pregnant. "You ready?"

"Can't someone else do all this? I don't care about the flowers or the fabric on the inside of her coffin."

"There is no one else." He wrapped his arms around me and pulled me close against his chest. "I'll help."

I leaned my head on his arm. How many times would this man hold me up? "Thank you."

He led me through the day, stopped to feed me when I'd forgotten to eat, answered questions I couldn't bring myself to think about, and brought me home after the sun dipped low in the sky. We'd met with The Friends Home, the funeral director, her attorney, and a real estate agent. Mama's house, which had sat empty on Marlton Road for weeks, was going to be put on the market tomorrow. Hopefully, the next family to live there would fill it with all the light and love my mother lacked in her later years.

I thought back to my childhood, to the time when my mother and her coven would hang clothes on the lines behind our houses. They'd drink lemonade and wear aprons full of clothespins, and the windows would be opened wide because none of us had air conditioning. When their husbands had all been preoccupied with the lawn or the baseball game, they'd take us by the hands and fly into the sky. Mama had been happy then. I'd swear to it.

Uncle Stump came through the side door without knocking. "I almost went to Auburn. I'm still not used to you guys being out here." He hugged me. Even with his gray hair and age spots all over him, he was handsome. Time had been kind to him.

"Nope. We're here."

"How are you?" He paused to examine me, and I took a deep breath.

"I'm okay."

"Well, you look like hell. I hope you're exhausted and slightly hungover, or else you need to make some changes."

"What is it with your generation? Can't you keep anything to yourselves?"

"We like to be clear, and don't lump me in with your mother. She was nasty."

"I know." Boy, did I know.

Thirty minutes later, he was snoring on the couch, which wasn't surprising. Uncle Stump always took a nap after arriving. I leaned against the counter in my kitchen, listening to the soft rumblings of his breathing and staring at the lake behind our house. There had to be a way out of this. She was dead, and I wished the curse had died with her.

I dragged myself up the stairs and fell onto my own bed. Uncle Stump was right. I was exhausted. Tomorrow I'd be a little hungover, and I'd bury the woman who raised me.

When I woke, the aroma of homemade spaghetti sauce filled the house. Isaiah always loved when Uncle Stump came to town. He said his cooking was almost as good as his stories. I showered, brushed my teeth, blew out my hair, and found a summer dress in my closet. I wasn't the one who'd died.

"There she is," Uncle Stump said as I joined the rest of my family in the kitchen. They were all in motion with him at the center of the hive. Isaiah was chopping onions, Gwen was washing a head of lettuce, and Ike was pulling wine glasses out of the china cabinet.

"I think you should stay here. Don't go back to Arizona." He was a bright light from my past. The funny uncle who made even my mother laugh. We needed him in Alloway with us.

"Absolutely not. The winters here depress me." He poured wine into the glasses Ike placed on the table. "I miss the people, though." He filled five glasses.

"They can't have wine. They're not twenty-one."

"Nonsense." He tipped his head to Ike. "He can join the army, carry a rifle, and kill someone in another country, but he can't have some wine with dinner?"

"Well, she's only seventeen."

He handed a glass to Gwen. She delighted in the offer. "And she can fly and set this whole town on fire. I think we can trust her with some vino."

"You're a terrible influence."

"I was innocent until your mother and her friends got to high school and corrupted me." He flashed me that rueful smile that reminded me of why he'd been married and divorced four times.

"Were they fun?" I pleaded with him to tell me, even if it was a lie. "I can't remember Mama as anything but bitter."

"Oh, Lord. Those girls used to carry on. They were nothing *but* fun." He took a long sip of his wine. "When we were teenagers, I worshipped all of them. I couldn't decide which one of her friends I wanted to date first."

"Who won?" Isaiah asked him.

"Not me. Clara would have hurt me bad if I'd touched one of them. Relationships with witches are not to be taken lightly."

"Amen," Ike and Isaiah said at the same time, and my family was engulfed in laughter.

This was what it should have been like. I thought of calling Sloane's and inviting all of them over. They always loved Uncle Stump as much as I did, but I couldn't ask Helene to come here. She was tortured just by having us all together in Auburn for a short time. The house that Isaiah and I lived in together would be too much.

"Was Daddy scared to date Mama?" I asked.

"Your father was a brave man, because Clara was never easy." I took my own sip of wine. God, that woman had been difficult. "But he loved her." He shook his head as if he couldn't believe how lucky my mother had been. "Worshipped her, really." Isaiah put his glass on the table and scraped the onions into the pan on the stove. He noticeably didn't turn around. "The night he died, we were all standing around his bed waiting for it. The cancer had eaten him from the inside out and was starting to work on his brain." I missed Daddy. "He told your mother that he'd lived a thousand lives the first night she let him kiss her, and that he'd wait for her in heaven just to kiss her again."

I closed my eyes and let the tears spill over. It was easy to forget after he left how much Mama had been loved. Each day she'd lived without him, she'd grown colder. Gwen dropped spaghetti into the boiling water, while Ike searched for silverware in the drawer. The words were just old stories to them. To me, it was the soul of my mother. Her essence she'd let be forgotten.

Isaiah was staring at me when Uncle Stump added, "I guess when you've truly loved someone the way your father loved your mother, death is nothing, because you've already had it all."

"I'm going to go make sure the canoes are far enough off the water," Isaiah said and walked out of the room without another word. He left me empty. The same way he'd found me so many years ago.

We listened to Uncle Stump's stories throughout dinner. He kept filling his glass as I let myself get lost in his tales. He'd never been so open about my mother's coven when she'd still been alive, and she'd *never* been open.

We cleaned the table, and I put the boxes of old albums in the center of it. I needed to select pictures to be displayed at the funeral home, but the majority of them had been taken before I was even born. In some of them, it took me a few minutes to recognize my mother.

"She's so happy," I said, staring at the woman surrounded by her three best friends. Their bodies were tight and powerful, their smiles bright and eyes shining. They were brilliant even in the black-and-white photographs. "And they look so strong."

Uncle Stump took the picture from my hand and stared at it. "That Poppy." He shook his head. "She was the one." He tipped his head toward the photo. "That red hair I've been chasing for fifty years since."

"You're terrible."

"That woman had a razor-sharp wit, too. I *loved* it."

"I remember how bold she was. Sloane is the same way."

"Poppy was never scared of the Virago."

I'd never heard him mention them, but usually my mother was around when he visited. "Were the others?"

He laid the photo down between us and picked up another from the box. "The other three were cautious. Poppy was fearless. That's why that coven from Upper Pittsgrove came to her first for help."

"What coven?"

"Before you were born, there were many more witches in the area. Good and bad, but the Virago was picking off witches from the Upper Pittsgrove coven. Their Earth witch died in a car accident. Your mother never thought it was an accident." This was the first time I was hearing any of this. "And the fire witch moved away." He looked to the ceiling as if his memory were stored there. "The story was she'd gotten pregnant and was sent away, but I never did hear the rest of it."

"What happened?"

"The Upper Pittsgrove witches came to Auburn one night and I was the one to open the door. I'd graduated two years before, but

I still liked those Upper Pittsgrove girls."

"Does every story with you revolve around the women in it?"

"I'm an old man. Leave me alone."

"Go on." I needed to know what the Virago did. What I'd avoided these last two decades.

"The witches came over. Your mother's coven was whole. They could cast a spell. The Upper Pittsgrove coven needed protection. They were alone and under attack. Fires, skirmishes while flying, one of their fathers was killed in a tractor accident. It went on and on."

"Where were their mothers?"

"I don't know." He stared at the wall and shook his head, trying to remember. "They went home with the witches and cast some spell to make Upper Pittsgrove sacred ground like Auburn. It seemed harmless enough. Just creating a few boundary lines."

"That's why I belong in Auburn."

Uncle Stump stared at me, and it felt as if he knew that my reasons for wanting to go back were more than just protection. "Well, it didn't work. Graduation night, they both drowned down at the Elmer Lake. Their bodies were found on the bank just past the Upper Pittsgrove line."

I gasped. Disgusting Virago. Killing them on graduation night. "What happened to the other one? The witch who moved away?"

"Don't know. Never heard another word about her. Her last name was Sickler. That's all I remember." He smiled a little. "That and her legs were as long as my hopes she'd dance with me."

With Uncle Stump in town, I could take a few minutes and laugh. I forgot in that small glimpse of time that my mother had died, taking with her any hope of healing my coven. Since he was a man, he wasn't privy to the inner working of the coven, but he was still hilarious to listen to.

The following morning, the sun shone bright and blared through the car windshield all the way to the funeral home. When I reached my spot in the room where I would stand at the head of the receiving line, Isaiah handed me a glass of water, which I drank in deep gulps, and then he settled to my right. A silent pillar of support.

There weren't many people left in this town who knew my mother, but all of the residents of Auburn came to pay their respects. They always would. No matter how far away Mama moved or for how long she'd been gone, they'd come to her funeral if they could get there. Sloane, Lovie, and Helene sat in the third row while their girls took Gwen for a much-needed break in the sitting room across the hall. From where I stood, I could see the way they leaned into each other as they stood in a circle. I watched them with the same curiosity I had at Gwen's birthday party. Would they have been any different if they'd known each other the last seventeen years? Ever put her hand on Gwen's back as Gwen rested her head on Maya's shoulder, making it seem as if they hadn't missed a moment. I turned to face my coven. Many moments had been missed between the four of us, but they were here, and that should be all that mattered.

Isaiah helped his mother in to pay her respects. I didn't think she'd ever liked Mama. I wasn't even sure she liked me. My suspicions were confirmed when she saw Helene and gushed all over her about how pretty she still looked and how she never stopped missing her. Helene was gracious as she hugged her. I caught myself wondering who'd be standing next to me if I hadn't married Isaiah. If there was a man out there I'd missed out on because I'd been too sad to see anything or anyone.

The service ended. Every attendee filed out into the sunshine, leaving me and Gwen staring at my mother in her casket. I held Gwen's hand.

"Mimi said she loves you," Gwen said.

I squeezed her hand tighter. "When did she say that?"

"Just now." Gwen hugged my paralyzed body and followed the

others out the front door to their cars.

What else do you have to say, Mama? I glared at her body. She could have spoken to me the same way she had to Gwen, but she'd chosen not to. *Tell me.* There was nothing but silence . . . and love. I could feel it everywhere around me. I slipped a picture of her coven in all its glory between her and the silk liner of her casket. *They'll forgive you like their daughters forgave me.* I waited for her to say something. Anything. I stepped back and let my hand fall to my side. It was the last time I'd see her. *Tell Daddy I said hi,* I thought and then walked out into the bright sunshine.

We followed the hearse to the graveyard. An even smaller crowd joined us there. Each of us threw a white carnation on the top of my mother's casket. My hopes that she'd reverse her horrible curse were thrown away with the petals. When they began to lower her casket into the ground, a cool breeze swept across my face. I turned to face it and saw Lovie and Sloane and Helene walking the path out of the cemetery. Their hope was gone, too.

X

No one can make you brave.
You're born with that power.

PRESSED THE TOWELS INTO the carpet with my feet. Gwen did a cartwheel on the lawn below our bedroom window. She twirled around and pulled the water from the lake over her head. She was beautiful, and she was powerful. At the sound of the doorbell, I abandoned my drying job and tossed the wet towels onto the bathroom floor to wait until I returned.

Ever was standing on the other side of the door, looking as if she might fall to her knees and cry at the sight of me. "I need to talk to you."

I grabbed her by the arm and led her inside as I looked back to see if she was alone. I swung the door closed with my foot and took her into the kitchen. I'd officially met her only weeks ago, but the topics we could discuss ranged from life to death, celebration to tragedy. "Sit." I motioned to a chair by the table and pulled one over to be near her. "Can I get you something to drink?"

Ever shook her head, barely acknowledging I'd offered her anything. Water splashed across the closed windows behind us. It sounded like a fire hose dousing the house, which managed to grab Ever's attention.

"It's Gwen," I explained. "She's enamored with her influence over the elements. She's been having water fun all morning, and she's very unpredictable. She soaked two carpets before I got all the windows shut."

Ever's laugh broke through the dismal aura she'd brought through the front door with her, but just as abruptly, something shifted, and her cloud returned. She stared at the table between us.

She was different from her mother—at least around me. Ever wasn't swift with her actions. She was more calculated in her responses. "What is it, Ever?"

She inhaled and faced me. The tortured look in her eyes betrayed the pain she'd brought with her that she was trying to hide. "I thought . . . maybe because you barely know me . . . and because—" She choked a little on her words. "He's your son who might die, that you'd help me."

Of course I'd help her. I reached out and held her hands. "I am trying to help, Ever. I swear I am."

"I know." I believed her, which was why I had no understanding of what she was saying. "I actually was hoping you'd help me change myself to stop it."

What she was suggesting prickled at the back of my neck. It was a dull thud lodged behind my ears before it even fully came to my understanding. "Change? How?"

"If I wasn't a witch anymore, I wouldn't be part of the coven. And without the coven, the curse won't apply to me." I thought she was going to cry, and yet strength oozed from her like hot lava from a volcano. "And it won't apply to Ike."

I released her hands, ready to kill someone. "Does Ike know you're here?" I leaned back in my chair, annoyed. I'd beat my son if he were a part of this.

She shook her head.

I moved my chair closer and took Ever's hands in my own. She had to hear every word I was about to say. If I left her with nothing else, this would be enough. "I do know you, Ever. You are my sister's daughter, and I love you like my own." Tears fell from her eyes, and I wiped them away the same way I would have Gwen's. "But even if that weren't true . . . *never* give up your powers for a man. Never." The water drenched the window again behind us. "Any man worth such a gesture would never allow it."

"It's the only way." Her voice cracked. She was losing her resolve.

"Ever, I don't know what your not being a witch would do to this coven. To your sisters. Our family. But even if there were no consequences for anyone but you, you can't do it. Would you ever give up Ike?"

Tears filled her eyes again. "No."

"Then why give up yourself?" She lowered her head at my words, and I pulled her to me and held her close until she calmed.

"Mrs. Kennedy." Her voice and her posture were solid. "I love Ike more than the air and the sky and the sun and the moon. I love Ike more than I love being a witch, and if I have to give that up to save him, then I will." Her lip quivered as she added, "I can't lose him."

Ever's proclamation tore at my heart. I believed every word she was saying and knew I'd never felt the same thing. The love for my children was different from the way I felt about my husband. Isaiah was my friend and he was my partner, but I didn't love him more than being a witch. This young girl in front of me made me long for something I didn't realize I'd lost out on until her mother had returned to town.

"Come with me," I said and stood. I grabbed my purse and keys off the counter by the sink.

"Where are we going?"

I took one last deep breath before committing to this horrible plan. "To unleash the hounds of hell. God help us." I tore through the house, gaining power with every step. This was right. It took Ever coming to my house to remind me of the things worth risking it all for. "Hey, crazy Earth witch!" I yelled as we walked out of the garage. "Let's go."

"Where are we going?" Gwen asked as she jogged over to join us.

"To Auburn," I said.

Ever stepped out from behind me, and Gwen's expression filled with love. "For what?"

"To change history, and we're going to need you."

"I'm in," Gwen said and climbed in the back seat of the car.

Ever stood next to the car, confused.

"You can sit up front, Ever."

I glanced over at her several times while we drove the Woodstown-Alloway Road. Her head leaned on the car window, and her gaze was lost in the sky. I looked up through the front windshield and watched the storm clouds rush into formation above us. "Was it supposed to rain today?" I feared Ever's visit had somehow set a storm in motion.

"It was supposed to be sunny," Gwen answered. She was disappointed the rain would ruin her plans. "Ever, you should see how good I'm getting." She took her seatbelt off and leaned over the front seat. "Today, I lit a fire, added air until it was raging, and then moved water from the lake to put it out."

"All without burning down our house," I said proudly. I tried to focus on everything but the clouds above us.

"Mostly. The corner on Ike's side doesn't count."

I made Gwen rebuckle, but they continued chatting about her new powers. No one seemed to be listening, not even the person speaking.

We pulled into Auburn, and the severe worry lifted. I was still aware of the sky and the past and the moment in which I decided to let go of the future to live in the present, but my powers grew stronger with every inch the car moved toward Sloane's house. Each member of the household—my sisters—were waiting for us in the yard when we arrived. Ever turned to me, wondering if I'd been in contact with them.

"Something like this, they could sense." The way I felt right now, it was hard to believe every person in the town couldn't tell something unearthly was about to go down.

"Oh."

We piled out of the car and walked straight to where everyone was standing. They all looked to me for an answer. "I'm willing to try if you guys still want to," I said. I should have said it the first night we'd all been together.

"Are you sure? You might be completely right. This could destroy us all," Helene said, and I prayed she was wrong.

I glanced over my shoulder at Ever. "It will definitely destroy us if we don't. We have no other choice."

"We'll need a spell," Helene said to Sloane.

The wind kicked up, swirling around us. It was a warning, and we all ignored it. Our choice had been made, and not a single one of us was willing to turn back.

"I already have it." We followed Sloane into the house. "I wrote it twenty years ago and have been tweaking it since we moved home."

Lovie and Sloane removed the leaves from the kitchen table and pushed it to the side, leaving about six square feet in the center of the kitchen for us.

"When you guys created Carl, how did you do it?" Sloane asked the girls. I still couldn't believe the girls had chosen to turn a stuffed animal into a living one with their first spell. I noted the dog was cowering under the table. He was smart to trust his instincts.

Maya, Ruby, and Ever hesitated, but Gwen jumped right in. "We stood in a circle, held hands, and recited the spell."

"What spell?" Sloane asked.

"Ruby wrote it."

Sloane looked proudly at her daughter.

"I pretty much copied the failed bird spell."

"I'm still proud," her mother said.

The girls moved into a circle facing out toward their mothers and held hands. The reality was kicking in. My breaths were shallow. I could feel my mother rolling over in her grave. She would have killed us all for this. Witches or not.

"I'm going to give each of you the spell to begin. You are the future, and you're innocent," Sloane said. I was jealous of their innocence. I hoped today we were preserving it. "I'm going to give it to you in your minds."

The girls nodded and closed their eyes. Gwen's face lit up, signifying she could see the words. I waited and watched for all those years, and ever since she realized her powers, it seemed like only a blink of an eye. "Cool!" Gwen yelled.

"How did you do that?" Ruby asked.

"Magic, of course." Sloane laughed, but the thunder rumbled above us, followed by streaks of lightning illuminating the dark room. The world outside was a deep charcoal color. The new leaves on the trees threatened to all blow away along with the branches holding them.

"Okay. Let's start. Close your eyes. Concentrate. Believe what you can do to affect change." Gwen's head fell back as she lifted her chin toward the ceiling at the same time her sisters did. "Breathe in your power." They were a gloriously cohesive unit. "Now recite the spell."

What once was four, can never be three
A force united to set them free

The unspoken truth of loss and fear
Hidden by hope, the answer lies here

Forgiveness and love, repair the tragic past
Betrayal, desertion, the spell that was cast

Twenty years apart. Too long to mourn
Now right the wrong that hatred had born

Our daughters held hands and spoke the words of the spell to the universe. They repeated it, letting thunder punctuate each line. Gwen winced as the wind beat against the side of the house.

"Don't stop!" I yelled over the noise of the storm.

What once was four, can never be three . . .

The front and back doors flew open, and the wind blew around us. The girls' hair blew across their faces. I wanted to cover them with something, but nothing would be more protective than their four mothers together holding hands.

Forgiveness and love, repair the tragic past . . .

The couch slid across the floor and toward the doorway of the kitchen. I threw it off its track, and it lodged in the doorway. Every item from every shelf or tabletop was darting through the air. The front and back doors banged against their hinges. The storm was inside with us. We were running out of time. Sloane, Lovie, Helene, and I formed a circle around our daughters and held hands for the first time in twenty years. Two full covens. The walls shook. Broken glass and dishes swirled at our feet. I closed my eyes, unable to see through the winds' ravages. I chanted, even as the dark bass of the thunder drowned out everything but the spell that kept falling from our lips.

What once was four, can never be three
A force united to set them free

The unspoken truth of loss and fear
Hidden by hope, the answer lies here

Forgiveness and love, repair the tragic past
Betrayal, desertion, the spell that was cast

Twenty years apart. Too long to mourn
Now right the wrong that hatred had born

Then, almost as quickly as the storm took hold, it was gone. The wind stopped blowing, and the sky calmed. The house was held in a heavy silence. Not one of us moved.

"We did it. It's gone. I can feel it's gone," Helene said, but I was already inhaling the fresh air.

"I can, too," Lovie said a moment before Sloane's confirmation came as well.

The house was in shambles. The front door was hanging off the hinges. Pictures of Lovie and Sloane and Helene were lying on the floor in broken frames. I held Gwen in my arms. I was whole for the first time since I'd been eighteen, maybe even before that. After Sloane and Helene's mothers had died, I'd never felt the same about anything, including myself. In the next breath, I wished Ike was there with us, too.

"Ike." He was at work . . . on a farm. The storm could have killed him. "I have to find Ike." I turned following my panic toward the back door.

"He's okay," Ever said. "He went in the Hitchners' basement.

He said the damage isn't too bad over there."

I stopped and stared at my son's girlfriend. "Ever, how did you talk to him?"

Her eyes darted to her mother and back at me. "Well . . . see . . . Ike seems to have some powers."

"What?" All of us stopped what we were doing.

"He can hear me . . . in his head. He can also talk back."

"How?"

She shook her head, comfortable in the innocence of the truth. "No idea. It's never happened to me before, but I'm guessing it has something to do with his mother being a witch."

"And it has something to do with you." Gwen pointed at Ever. "He can't hear anyone else unless you're involved. It's something special between the two of you. I've tried it on Dave Anzaldo a hundred times, and he never hears a word I say." I laughed a little at my adorable daughter. "Of course, that's when I'm actually talking to him, too."

"Did you check on Isaiah?" Lovie asked. I turned to Helene, expectant. It took a minute for me to realize Lovie was talking to me. I shook my head in disgust. With that one question, Lovie made me realize that, even after twenty years, I'd never loved Isaiah as my own. It wasn't fair to him. It was only partially his fault, but it was both of our lives. I didn't even care where he was. I was the worst wife in the world. "I was only worried about Ike." Isaiah deserved better. "I have to go." I had to find my husband. "Gwen, stay and help everyone clean up. I'll be back if I can."

Helene grabbed me by the arm. "Are you okay?"

"I'm better than I've been in twenty years."

She pulled me into a hug and said the only word left that would bind me to her forever. "Geesey."

"I love you, Helene."

"What else can we do?" Gwen's voice rose from the rubble.

Sloane, Lovie, and Helene's heads snapped up and stared at her. Gwen scared them. She was new and unpredictable.

"Nothing without my permission," I said. That poor child had so much to learn.

The fire whistle blew from down the street. The power was gone. Through the open back door I could see half the trees were lying on the ground. Lovie's car was flipped on its side.

"We've done enough," Ever said.

We all had a lot to learn. I left them and raced home to find my husband.

We'd forget it all for love.

I TOOK THREE STEPS OUT the back door and flew to my house. I tore through the kitchen, living room, and bedrooms, but Isaiah wasn't home. The need to talk to him had grown urgent on the flight back to Alloway. Clarity was an adrenalin rush. I spread my palms out wide in front of me. The energy was lost from my fingertips, but I was still whole. We'd not only cast a spell but also overturned one.

I disappeared and inhaled the presence of my powers. It was as if I'd never lost them. Flying, disappearing, moving things, it had all returned with a vengeance, but it was different from what I remembered. We were mighty and invincible. I wanted to set the couch on fire just to watch it burn, but Isaiah would kill me.

He walked through the living room, yelling all our names. I showed myself in the family room and nearly scared him to death. "Don't do that. How many times have I told you not to do that?"

Frustration mixed with fear sprung from him. "Where are the kids?"

"Ike's at work. He's okay." I looked at my husband. It was the first time in a long time that I was really seeing him. He was exhausted and weary. There wasn't a hint of how his eyes lit up when he smiled. I just remembered telling him how they had the first time we'd been together. The weekend Helene had gone away.

He turned, searching behind him, and asked, "What about Gwen?"

"She's in Auburn. Where we belong." Isaiah stared back at me as though it was his first time seeing me, too. His gaze fell from my eyes to the floor at my feet. A scowl settled on his face. He was equally as unimpressed. "When I say 'we,' I mean Gwen and me."

"What are you talking about?" He found me ridiculous. He had so many times over the past two decades, but we were all the other had. In some strange way, we'd learned to love each other for it. We didn't have to tell someone new about our sordid past. There were no secrets between Isaiah and me, only a history of death. The first thing we'd killed was his and Helene's love. The second was Helene's and my sisterhood.

"Isaiah, if you could do this all over again, would we be together?" We'd never come close to these words. "If that one night had never happened, what would your life be?"

A silence fell on my husband. Settled in the lines on his face was the same expression of serene resolve he had whenever he took the canoe out on the lake. He almost looked like he loved me. "We can't change the past, Gisel." There was a kindness in Isaiah that wasn't completely extinguished even after losing his only true love.

None of it swayed me. I'd been leading Isaiah into decisions our entire adult lives. I'd take him down this path, too. "We don't have to keep going this way. We can right the wrong, even if we can't change the past."

"I don't understand what you're saying." He circled around me with his head tilted. He wasn't the dense idiot my mother had always claimed he was. "Helene hates me. It was twenty years ago. There's nothing left of that, and we have two kids together."

"And I love you because of them, but there's a part of me that hates a part of you." Not a hint of surprise showed on his face, because he was the only person in the world who understood exactly what I was saying. "When I lie awake in the middle of the night, that part tells me how horrible we were." The tears were going to come. My cheeks burned with the heat ahead of their arrival. "It creeps into my thoughts when I drive anywhere near Auburn." I threaded my fingers together in front of me. "When I watched Gwen with her friends at her birthday party, that part of me hated you."

His steely eyes fixed on me. "There were two of us that night."

"I hate myself, too." I walked over to my husband and wrapped my arms around his waist. His hung at his sides. "No matter how much I love you, I'll never forgive you for being the worst mistake of my life." He held me away from him. "I've waited twenty years. Helene's forgiven me, and I still can't shake the little voice in the back of my mind that says we're awful."

"You're not making sense, Gisel. It's been a long day." He stepped away from me and ran his hand through his hair. He stared out the window at the lake.

"No. It's been a long life." I'd faced the truth of our marriage, and there wasn't a doubt in my mind that Isaiah felt the same.

He left his memories of the lake and turned to face me. "Gisel—"

"Isaiah." I breathed in the truth. "I want to love someone more than the air and the sky and the sun and the moon."

BONUS MATERIAL

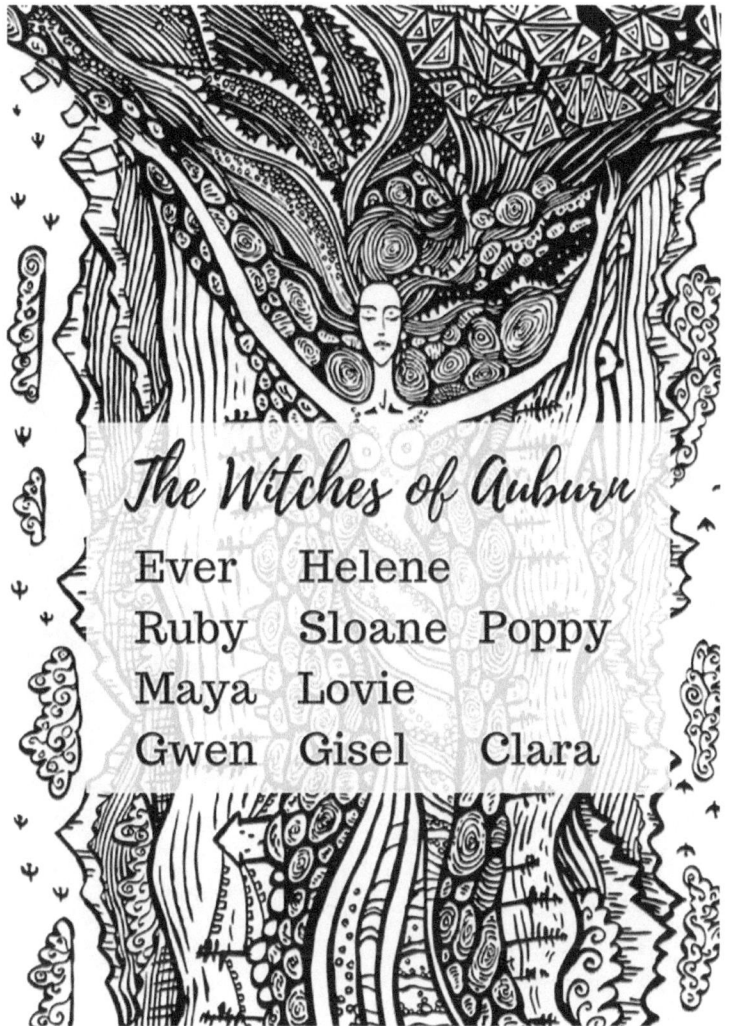

The Witches of Auburn

Ever	Helene	
Ruby	Sloane	Poppy
Maya	Lovie	
Gwen	Gisel	Clara

The Kingsway Coven

Jennifer
Maryann
Riley
Tara Jane

Please see the next page for a preview of
the next installment in The Witches of Auburn series.

THE WITCHES OF AUBURN

BOOK TWO

The Sins of Our Fathers

HAZEL BLACK

Ever

I FLEW HIGH OVER THE railroad tracks and Alloway Lake. Ike and I spent the last day before he left for school canoeing the lake. We'd laughed at how good it felt to be out in the sunlight, together, and not have to hide our relationship. We didn't speak of the curse that caused our parents' history, or the fact that he wouldn't be at Woodstown High School when my senior year began in a few weeks.

I turned west toward Cumberland County and dipped down closer to the woods on the other side of Upper Pittsgrove. The Dead Field was right below me. I banked left and flew in a large circle, taking in the area from above. I was sure it was the barren field below, but the patch of land beneath me was in ruins. I landed and grabbed a handful of soil, letting it trickle through my fingers. Remnants of stems and stalks covered the ground, but their dull gray color melded into the diseased land beneath them.

I need to see you. Ike's voice warmed me. I wasn't sure "need" described how I felt about him. It was scarily close to an obsession.

You just saw me last night.

Can you come back tonight?

I'd already spent too much time at Rowan University. Ike was exhausted from football and the heat. He fell asleep every time I was there, which I didn't mind, but he needed a good night's rest more than he needed to see me.

Why are you not answering yes?

I knew he was laughing at me.

The wind swirled around low to the ground, and I tilted my head, listening. Murmured chatter slipped on the tips of the breeze as it blew toward me from the other side of the field.

Shh. Someone is coming. I needed him to be quiet so I could concentrate and listen.

Who? Where are you?

I'm at the Dead Field thinking of you.

"I don't know what happened." The voice was across the field in front of me. I stayed safely invisible in my spot.

"It's finally displaying why it's called dead field. The arsenic caught up to the flowers."

The woman's short curly hair barely moved as she shook her head in dismay. She put her hands on her stout hips and stared at the ground. "That makes no sense. The tests said the soil make-up is the same. Why would things start dying now?"

"I don't know," the man said. "But the way it looks makes more sense than all those flowers blooming. It used to make me crazy. We couldn't build on the land or farm it, but those flowers taunted me every season."

"Only you could be taunted by a field full of wildflowers." The man took a step closer to the woman and kissed her neck. They were old enough to be my grandparents.

"You better behave."

Are they gone? I wish I could read your mind.

I rolled my eyes at Ike's impatience.

Just hold on a minute.

"Or what?"

"Or those flowers won't be the only thing taunting you," she teased and walked back the way she came with the man following close behind.

I stayed silent and invisible, still concentrating on the tainted soil that had somehow found a way to defeat the warrior flowers. The hair on my arms stood, my ears strained to pick up any miniscule sound, and a chill slipped across my chest. I wasn't alone, but this was Upper Pittsgrove. I shouldn't have had to worry.

Air whooshed by me, moving in the same direction the couple had gone.

Ruby. Where are you?

Why? Even though she answered, it was pretty clear she wasn't interested in talking.

I need your help in Upper Pittsgrove. I tried to sound nonchalant. No one even knew I was there, but the sense that something was about to happen crawled down the back of my throat and formed a lump that lodged there.

Are you okay? Because I kind of can't ask Sam to take his hand off my boob, tell him I'm a witch, and disappear to come find you . . . but I will if you need me to.

I'm fine. Not sure I can say the same for this couple that is with me.

Call Gwen. She's in Alloway helping her mother move their stuff to our house.

I followed the breeze past an ancient farmhouse abandoned in favor of a dated colonial on the edge of the property and then stopped and listened.

"What should we do to them? Electrocution? We haven't done that in a while." I could barely hear the voices and wasn't sure I was correctly making out what was being said. Electrocution? I moved again, slowly and barely impacting the air as I stayed focused on the voices around me.

"I can't find the peanut butter," the man inside the kitchen said.

"We are definitely not out of peanut butter," his wife answered from the bedroom. She was folding his undershirts with the windows opened wide.

"Well, I can't find it," he practically mumbled under his breath.

"Robbery? Double suicide?" The whispers came again. The cold, business-like way they discussed their afternoon activities in the presence of the victims was scarier than the ideas of what they might do. I was reminded of the cruel attack on my dog and the destroyed dress in my bedroom, which was child's play compared to what they were contemplating. The Virago didn't seek entertainment from the arts. They created havoc to combat their boredom.

"You are an idiot," the elderly woman called out to her husband. She dropped the shirt she had been folding onto her bed.

My heart raced in my chest. If she made it to the kitchen, I thought they'd both be killed. For what or in what way, I couldn't tell, but something dreadful was about to happen. I could feel it in my bones.

"Robbery. I'll go cut the phone line. We might be here for a while."

My spine straightened at the detached tone in the invisible voice. I crouched behind the corner of the house and waited for the air to divulge the witch's departure. The screen fell out of the bedroom window as the other one entered the house.

I followed the breeze to the pole by the street and circled around to the box.

"Who's there?" she said. There was no whispering this high in the air. "What do you want?"

"I could ask you the same?" I said over the pounding of my heart in my ears.

Ever, came Ike's voice in my head.

Not now.

I kept moving. Dodging what I assumed were her movements to determine exactly where I was located.

"Just enjoying the lovely afternoon. It's a shame you aren't going to be able to say the same." The air swept by a second before her arm was around my neck. "Your shadow betrays you." Her breath rushed across my ear as she said, "You're strong. Young." She twisted until the two of us were above the road.

"Stronger than you," I said and pried her arm off me. I held her wrist between both hands and used her as a counter weight as I swung us in the air. Like a figure skating pair, we soared in a circle with me leaning back, her arm firmly in my grasp. An eighteen-wheeler approached. I calculated the time until its arrival and on our last rotation, I released her and launched myself high into the air. She appeared, hit the truck between its headlights, and was thrown into the ditch on the side of the road.

The witch lay in the dirt, moaning, but she was alive. Her left leg was mangled. She grasped it before disappearing again. The tractor trailer pulled to the side of the road, and I flew back to the house and into the open window.

"What was that?" the woman yelled from the kitchen. She wasn't talking about the collision out front, though. The dresser drawers in her bedroom were being searched and slammed shut one by one.

I landed next to the dresser and closed the drawer that had just opened.

"What the—"

"Your friend needs you," I whispered to the invisible evil beside me. Her breath caught in jagged shock. "You'd better hurry. She ran into something trying to cut the phone line."

"Why, what is going on in here?" The woman surveyed her ransacked bedroom. I followed the breeze out the window and waited outside. "Dear Lord. Stanley, get in here. Someone tried to rob us."

"Maybe they took the peanut butter," he said, but as he came to a stop in the doorway, his mouth hung open at the sight of his bedroom. "Call 9–1-1."

"I was just in here," she said and dialed the phone next to their bed.

Ever!

I'm sorry. There's a lot going on here. There's been a robbery.

At your house?

No. I'm still in Upper Pittsgrove. The truck driver was searching the ditch and the fields on both sides of the street. He'd felt the impact but never saw what he'd hit. He turned back, inspected the front of his truck, climbed back into the cab, and drove off a moment before the police cruiser arrived at the couple's house.

I waited near the pole by the road, still invisible, and listened to the witches beside me.

"I think my leg is broken."

"How did you get hit by a truck?"

"I didn't get hit by it, some crazy witch threw me into it."

"Who was she?"

They couldn't feel me and had no idea I was there.

"Who knows? This whole area has been a yawn since that Auburn crew came back. It's like they're starting a movement or something."

"We have to get you out of here."

"I can't fly."

"Stay here. I'll fly home and get the car."

"Pathetic," she whispered under her breath.

I waited until she was loaded into the car and driven away. The couple thanked the trooper for coming and walked him outside. They discussed deadbolts and window locks and the alarm system they were going to have installed. Once I was sure the couple was safe, I flew home to find my mother and Ike waiting for me in the kitchen.

"I'm okay," I responded to both their aggressive stances and wide-eyed glares. "I swear. It was just a little issue."

"What happened? Exactly?" my mother asked. Ike seemed happy to let her be the interrogator.

"I was out flying and looking around. I landed in a field by this older couple's house."

"What older couple?"

"I have no idea who they are." My mother exhaled her frustration with the situation. "I was about to leave, but then felt two witches pass me, so I followed them. When I heard what they were planning to do, I had to step in."

"How did you know they were witches?"

"They were invisible. I knew they were evil by the things they were saying."

"Like what?"

I hesitated to weigh my possible answers. The situation had to have been significant enough to warrant me ignoring Ike's calls in my head but not dangerous to me personally, or else they'd both drive me crazy. Together and individually. "I thought they were going to rob them." My mother's head tilted to the side as if she didn't believe me. "Or maybe worse."

"Ever!" they both yelled at the same time.

"What did you want me to do? They seemed like a sweet old couple! I wasn't going to let something happen to them."

"Call me. Always, first, before you do anything else, call your mother."

I exhaled loudly, letting them both witness my depleting patience with this conversation. I may not have called my mom, but I called Ruby, which had to count for something. I wasn't about to bring her into this, though.

"I will. Next time. I promise."

"Where were you?"

"In Upper Pittsgrove. Right next to the field they call Dead Field."

My mother was lost in thought as she placed the location. "Off Friendship Road?"

"That's the one," Ike answered. I wasn't sure of the road exactly. I didn't travel via road names.

"But how is that possible? The Virago is not allowed in Upper Pittsgrove."

"I don't know, but they were there. One of them has a bum leg now." Her eyes widened until I thought they might pop out of her head.

"And how exactly did that happen?"

"She had a run-in with a tractor trailer." I got looks of incredulity from them both. "What? They were going to kill them. I couldn't let that happen." Her head fell back and her gaze focused on the ceiling as she squeezed her forehead between her thumb and middle finger.

"What's going on?" Ike's mother asked as she walked in the back door carrying a milk crate filled with random items and a hair dryer on top.

"Ever interrupted a crime in Upper Pittsgrove."

"Oh." Gisel turned her full attention to me. I wanted to somehow sneak upstairs with Ike and avoid this entire conversation.

"The criminals were invisible women who mentioned us."

"Really?" I didn't think her attention could increase, but yes, it could. "What did you do?"

"They separated, so I threw one of them into a truck and then told the other one to go help her."

Gisel's mouth hung open a little. "You talked to them?"

"As little as possible. They didn't see me."

Gisel handed my mother the crate and took the hair dryer from the top.

"We're not done talking about his," my mother said and followed Gisel up the stairs.

"She's right," Ike said. "We're not done. You cannot get into fights with the Virago." He moved closer to me and stared down. My eye contact never faltered. "You were outnumbered. No one knew where you were." I wrapped my arms around his neck. "You shushed me." I stood on my tiptoes and kissed his neck. "I'm serious, Ever. You have to be more careful."

"I promise."

"I don't believe you."

I kissed him again in a way that finished his argument.

HAZEL BLACK

HAZEL BLACK GRADUATED FROM RUTGERS University and returned to her hometown in rural South Jersey. Her mother encouraged her to take some time and find herself. After three months of searching, she began to bounce checks, her neighbors began to talk, and her mother told her to find a job.

She settled into corporate America, learning systems and practices and the bureaucracy that slows them. Hazel quickly discovered her creativity and gift for story telling as a corporate trainer and spent years perfecting her presentation skills and studying diversity. It was during this time she became an avid observer of the characters she met and the heartaches they endured. Her years of study taught her that laughter, even the completely inappropriate kind, was the key to survival.